A DIVERSIFIED BLACK WOMAN

VOLUME 1

I Feel So Blessed

SHAY 7

Library of Congress Control Number: 2011914091
ISBN 13: 978-0-615-51090-3
ISBN 10: 0-6155-1090-6

ShayTales

P.O. Box 115448
Atlanta, Georgia 30310
www.shaytales.com
Email us: rw4rp@shaytales.com

Cover photography, cover concepts, and book design by Shay 7
Cover design by Keith Saunders for MarionDesigns.com

DEDICATION

This book is dedicated to many people.

To God: I love you so much! While I am writing this tears come to my eyes because I get emotional when I am articulating my love for you. Your love is so amazing. It is the love I had been searching for all of my life. I feel great inside. I am truly complete. I know how to be happy without material things. I know how to love me unconditionally. It all started because I decided in my heart that I was going to be a living sacrifice for you. I gave you my "yes." However, you put it in my mind to say "yes" because I am chosen. You are my life. No more rubbernecking, you can drive me anywhere you want to go. I trust you. When I persevered during my trials, I showed you I loved you. When I held on when I couldn't see, I proved to you my loyalty. No matter how hot the fire became, I loved you. My loving you never failed and all things will work together for my good.

To Jesus: I play in my mind sometimes the pain you went through for me because I really want to understand. I don't ever want to forget because I never want to neglect what you have done for me. You have set me free in more ways than one! I watched the Gospel of John repeatedly. You are the paradigm I subscribe to be like every day. I love you.

To Holy Spirit: You guide me. You make sure that I am doing as God wants me to do. You direct me and keep me from making careless mistakes. With you I have great navigation. You speak to me and put things I need in my spirit. You are brilliant! I love and need you.

To Me: You loved me and lifted me up when I was feeling down. You encouraged me when it seemed there was no way out. I thank you for accepting God's will for our life. You stopped fighting and put God in our driver's seat. That was the decision that turned all wrong into right. I thank you for loving "me" and having unbelievable faith in God and our destiny. We were made to "fly."

To my mother Sweet "D": You support me more and more every day. I thank you for that. You are a blessing to my children and me. You made things easier for me just by being there when there was no one else physically there. I love you more than you will ever know. It has been a hard ride for me, but you stood right by my side. I am going to remain by your side, and one day take care of you how you have taken care of my children and me. We disagree sometimes, but our love for each other transcends any disagreement we have ever had. I love you mother.

To my sons Bradley and Jalen: The greatest job I have ever had and will have is being a mother. You two bring me great joy! You make me smile in the midst of any storm. I have dedicated you to God because he loves you more than I could ever love you. I know that as long as you are with him you will be okay. Allow his will to be done for your lives. I want you to always take care of each other. Always stand with your brother and keep him covered. Do not ever get so hung up on money that you cannot release it to help your brother. Let me pass on the word God gave me, "Own every one of your talents." This means create your own businesses—you are Kingdom Possessors. I love you.

To my sister Shuntay and my brother Boosie: I want the best for the both of you. Get what God has for you! I am here to help. You both have been wonderful to your nephews. They love the both of you as much as I do. I pray that we continue to grow stronger together. I'm paving the way. Look to God for directions. There is nothing special about me. God makes the difference. Moreover, God has a plan for you too. Always remember that <u>life is too great to live like it is too short</u>!

To my covenant brother and ex-husband Bradley: You have been there for me when I have needed you the most. You helped me unselfishly. I appreciate all that you have done for me without asking me any questions and without attaching any strings. With all that we have been through, it is wonderful to know you can count on me, and I can count on you.

To my aunt Carrie, my stepfather Rufus , my niece Cheka, my nephew Zay, my two great nephews, my uncles, my cousins, my church family (Touch of Life Prophetic Ministries International), Cynthia and Guy Griffin, LRT Properties, and my friends: I love you and appreciate every mark that you have made in my life. I need my family and friends. We may have our problems, but we must let love conquer all. A very special thanks to LRT Properties for the "grace" you bestowed upon my children and me during our time of need.

To Robert Walker (Bob): People often say blessings do not come to your doorstep. Well, if that is true, I feel beyond special because you came to my door. You have been a great blessing ever since the day I met you. When I give people my testimony about you, they are amazed. I thank God for you because you were a stranger that is truly a friend. You came through my brother, but you have been my angel too. What you have done for me, I know one day I will do for others. You have made an indelible impression on my life. Your love and charity has proven my faith in God to be true.

CONTENTS

"Rejection is simply an opportunity to make your own dreams come to life. Rejection is a no only when you refuse to turn it into a yes."

SPECIAL DEDICATION

To all my supporters and readers: Live the vision that God has given you. People will overtly and covertly try to kill it. They will converse about the decisions you make and say they are not wise. Yet, when you succeed they will be right by your side. Therefore, live the vision God has put in your heart. Sometimes you may have to take a risk and ignore all the naysayers. God will work everything out for those that love and trust him.

In memory of

My grandmother Emma (Mama) 2003
My aunt Yvonne 2001
My father Donald (Honkey) 1999
My aunt Trina 1996
My cousin James (Pnut) 1994
My cousin Bianca (BB) 1993

INTRODUCTION

Majority of the material in this book was written during 2000 and 2001. However, some new pieces were added after the birth of my second son in 2003 and immediately before the publication in 2011.

In 1999, I experienced a great depression that endured through 2002. In such a short period of time so much happened in my life. I felt as if all hell had broken loose. I feared a nervous breakdown. It was only by the grace of God that I survived. Years later, I realized that all pain is not bad pain. Sometimes it appears bad while you are experiencing it. However, some pains illuminate gifts. My writing was something I did for fun. I did not realize it was a gift until I experienced a cycle of trauma. My pains increased the intensity of my writing because writing proved to be therapeutic. After writing down my hurts and pains, I began to write poetry and stories that were beyond my experiences. I captured in words what I assumed someone else was incurring. I went from my hurts and pains, to channeling the pains and experiences of others, to a book. After my first book was completed—*A Diversified Black Woman Vol. 1*—I continued writing.

To keep me focused on living a great life, I would redundantly say, "Life is too short not to live and enjoy it." However, after much revelation I know that "life is too great to live like it is too short." When we live as if life is too short we have a proclivity to rush things. We fail to enjoy the journey. We fail to grab powerful lessons out of painful moments because we are focused more on the pain than the journey.

Even during painful times we have to muster up the strength to be the best people that we can. We are bound to discover extraordinary things about us and about the people that surround us amid our trials and tribulations. Trials and tribulations are dying and birthing times. While we grow and allow old things to die, we birth new and beautiful creations. When I was experiencing my trials and tribulations, I felt as if I were literally dying. I did not die, but there were things that were no longer vital to my life that died in me. This allowed a "new me" to resurrect.

We cannot resurrect if we continue to hold on to things that are no longer vital to us. If we refuse to let go of the things God wants us to let go of—whether they are relationships, idiosyncrasies, peccadilloes, material things, or mindsets—death is where we will remain. Dead people have no power. Powerless people cannot resurrect. Dead people cannot help anyone, but those who resurrect can save others.

Chapter One encapsulates my experiences. I have always been confident enough to share my truth with others. Some people do everything to keep their truth a secret. However, your truth is only a testimony when it is told.

Chapter Two is entitled "Fictional and Inspirational Section." It's flowing with poems that will inspire and entertain. There is a short story in this section—one of my favorites—"Candy Castles."

Chapter Three is the drama section. It contains poems that are about strong subjects such as rape, abuse, and homosexuality. I take the experiences of others and convey them into words. This section includes a short screenplay entitled *Damnation*. I was apprehensive about including this section; however, the greatest book of all—the Bible—is filled with stories that contain strong subject matters. Hence my apprehension dissipated quickly.

Chapter Four is entitled "Romance Section." It is not as extensive as the others. However, it is very unique. It encompasses poems of love and attraction from a man's and a woman's perspective.

This is not the average book a minister writes. I am a creative writer. I will write some self-help books someday. Nevertheless, I know there are "nuggets of wisdom" in this book that readers will not have to excavate.

"The times will change, but the recipe for a virtuous woman remains the same."

Chapter One

PERSONAL SECTION
(NONFICTION)

In this section, Shay 7 guides readers into her world. She writes about her experiences and people who have made a tremendous impact on her life. As with most books, reading the introduction is very important for the context of the material.

"Looking forward to an afterlife is asinine if you do not live life on earth to the fullest. Being a great steward requires us to do all that God has created us to do."

FIRST COMES MY CREATOR

Love is love
And you are my heart
Every breath I take—you give it to me
You are my soul
So deep
My spirit
COMPLETE
You are in the midst of my troubles
My guiding light
You hold my secret tunnel when things don't go so
right
Your creation I am
Your vessel to flow through
Love is love
And your love for me is proof!

"I'm not perfect, but every day I'm working towards
perfection as if it is obtainable. With God all things are
possible."

I'M BLESSED

Every day that I look around there seems to be
some type of test
Problems and pains in my life that causes me so
much stress
I pray and sometimes I don't understand my
storms
But I have to realize that without trials and
tribulations no wisdom could be born
Sometimes I get tired, and I just want to be happy
I can't understand why so much happens to me
But after a few years of spiritual growth and
understanding the concept of life
I appreciate all my sunshine, struggle, and strife
I realize that things will get hard
But what counts is that I hold on and call on the
Lord
Give God my problems and endure my tests
Because after it's all said and done **Shay realizes
that she is blessed!**

"I fail closer to success every day. I cannot have success
unless I fail first. There may be a lot of 'firsts' for me, but I
am appeased by knowing I have the victory."

GOD, CAN I WALK WITH YOU

I have always wanted to see
He who made me
Right here
Right now
On earth
In this life
I feel your spirit all the time
I hear you in my mind
If you came to me
Right now
Right here
This day
In flesh view
I would say, "God, can I walk with you?"
I know I may not have lived the way you wanted
me to
God, please have mercy and let me walk with you
God, I love you, and I have really tried
There were nights I felt I failed you, and I cried
Sometimes I didn't know what to do
But God can I walk with you?
I have tried so hard to do my best
To love—in flesh and spirit promote success
God, maybe you'll say I could have done better
I'll accept that and know that it's true
But God you know your daughter
I'm persistent
And I'll still ask boldly, **"God, can I walk with
you?"**
"If you don't know who you are in God, no one else will
believe you. They will also try hard to change your mind.
God can do more with us when we know who we are."

I FEEL SO BLESSED
(Titled poem)

Sometimes I guess I take things for granted
But every time I am writing my moments are
enchanted
God, I really thank you for the gift of being able to
express how I feel lyrically
Because to some it is a mystery
My writing—whether telling my soul or
entertaining—is my heart
And it feels so good to be able to open your heart
This is my gift
Therefore, it will be my bread and butter
Reading my writings take over me
I have to say that I am truly blessed
To write what I feel and release my stress
With something I truly love
For a long time I was looking for me
My writing was serendipity
Some people never find
What satisfies their souls or allows them to express
their minds
God, thank you
Did I tell you that?
Thank you because you know I looked over this
one for a while
**But even when I am dejected, writing makes me
smile.**

GOD, MAKE ME OVER

God, I just want you to make me over
Give me the beauty and favor of Queen Esther
The courage of Mordecai
The integrity of Job
The great counsel of Samuel
The heart of John
The zeal of Paul
The goodness of Noah
The faithfulness of Shadrach, Meshach, and
Abednego
The wisdom and wealth of Solomon
The loyalty of David
The boldness of Elijah
The ability to prophesy and work miracles like
Elisha
The obedience of Jeremiah
The ability to interpret dreams like Daniel
The forgiveness of Joseph
The blessings of Abraham
The meekness of Moses
The determination, faith, and bravery of Caleb and
Joshua
The chameleon ability of Isaiah
And the unconditional love, peace, and ability to
draw souls like Jesus
God, I need you
To-make-me-over!

WATCH ME DO ME

You can continue to converse about my failures
You can discuss how foolish I am
But when you talk about me, mention my strength
Speak about how I failed and got up again
You're supposed to be my friends
I see you cannot help hating on me
Your logic is tainted by bitterness
You have a negative propensity
Inside you are a mess
When I make it you'll say you knew I would
But you didn't know JACK
I am cognizant of you biting my back
You ol' enema
You can talk about me
I have no secrets
They are all in books
God warned me about people of your kind
People who will stay focused on my past and try to
poison my mind
And you think you have class
Classy people do not gossip about other people's
business all day
Classy people are too busy thinking of ways to get
paid
Tremendously sad
Outrageously bad
That you live your life as a Hater
Negative instigator
All you did was charge my battery
Your desire is to see me perspire
But it ain't happening
I'm calling you out

Ol' demon seed
You are the reason I fight like I do
If you stop hating on me, maybe you can see what
God has for you
I will not touch your innuendos
I know what you are spreading
You don't mean me well
I know wolves like you
It is not hard to tell
You will never stop me
Understand that!
And when you talk about me
You give me the wind to fly
I thank you because you push me into my destiny
You cause me to excel
So continue hating because it commands me to do
well
I am going to write, produce movies, and sing
I am going to do everything
That God has given me talent to do
The whole world shall believe
When they **watch-me-do-me!**

"God gives us all talents according to our abilities. Use what God has given you, and do not envy me. Proper use of your talent(s) will produce grace and victory." Matthew 25:14-30

Shay Seven

This speech is for the day that I accept my first huge award.

ACCEPTANCE SPEECH

Growing up there were times I didn't see
Anyone who believed or could feel my dreams—
just me
I lived in the ghetto, but I still had dreams
No real connections that would help me—at times
no way out it seemed
Still I believed
God, I became a woman—had troubles in and out
Caught up in the moments
Negativity all around
But when I reached out
God, you were there pulling the devil off my back
And placing me back on track
My trials and tribulations I don't regret
They have made me a woman no one will forget
Before everyone I am awarded this award because
of how I have been blessed
To God I give thanks for my family, my friends, my
talents, my trials, my determination, and my fans
that love ME
To God and the world I give my **ACCEPTANCE
SPEECH!**

Thank you for your support; I love you all.

CHAINS

God, I have been trying to break those **"CHAINS"**
since I was a little girl
I didn't want to be on welfare
So far I have never had to be
I didn't want to live in the projects as a woman
And you blessed me to leave with dignity
I never wanted to stand in line for food stamps
And I never did[1]
It wasn't that I thought I was too good
I knew there was more to life than just to live
Sometimes I needed assistance because I was in
need
But God I couldn't let those **"CHAINS"** shackle me
See, I took a look around and saw that my family
was poor
However, I am a new generation, and it is
incumbent upon me to knock down the prison
doors
I know I can do whatever I desire in life
Like everyone I'll have struggles, but it's worth the
fight
I remember getting onto a crowded bus with a
handful of pennies just to get to cosmetology
school
Who cares who laughed or snickered
No excuse was I going to accept to make me lose
Sometimes I went with bus fare going and no bus
fare to get back

---

[1]Since this poem, I have actually had to stand in line for food stamps. I was
ashamed; nevertheless, I had to realize it was a temporary situation that would
allow me to get to a better place in life. It was a very humbling experience.

God, I always prayed to get tips, and you made
sure I didn't lack
You saw how hard I tried; I had a husband
addicted to drugs in the streets
And a wonderful baby boy I had to feed
To finish school quickly, on some days I went from
nine to nine
I went through so much, but I was determined
"VICTORY" would be mine
Although I was blessed to break those **"CHAINS"**
A lot of people didn't make it
A lot of them believed they had nothing to gain
I don't want to hear the psychiatrist philosophy
I was there
I know if you don't have faith in God, it's hard to
get out, and you stay inside with no room to think
A lot of us can't help the hand we were dealt
Some of us can't control the hate we felt
See, people with silver and gold spoons in their
mouths can say what they want
They don't understand that sometimes it's hard to
break those **"CHAINS"** when they are linked to
generations of your family
When you see everyone else chained you figure
that's how life supposed to be
GOD, I just give thanks to you for allowing me to
see
Those **"CHAINS"** became broken when I realized
the strength from **JESUS** that I possessed in **ME!**

"It's hard to cover up your wings when you are made to
fly, so I say why try. I am going to fly and fly high."

MY LIFE STORY

When I was fourteen, you were the apple of my
eye
We became a couple, and when I turned fifteen
every weekend you were by my side
Waited for me to relinquish my virginity
Brought me happiness and spoiled me
Bought all my school clothes when you knew I got
paid like you
You were very good to me, and for you there was
nothing I wouldn't do
I married you at the age of sixteen
You were not legally a man yet—only eighteen
But you loved me, and I loved you
We were soul mates, and our love was true
Wherever you were, there was me
You were your left and I was your right butt-cheek
That's just how tight we were
We soon made and gave birth to a beautiful son
We were scared, but God's work was done
You started selling drugs, and I begged you to stop
You sweet-talked me time and time again
After you make a little more money, you promised
it would end
It never did
"Look, we have a son," I said
"I don't want his father back in jail or somewhere
dead"
You tried hard to see my plan
But things got even harder, and for you it was
difficult being a man
You started doing drugs, and I never even knew
It was my mother who had the clue

Shay Seven

She told me, and my heart dropped
Without telling what my mother said, I watched
your behavior myself and asked you to please stop
You denied it until I caught you in the act
I was so hurt, and I fought to get you back
But going to school and taking care of our baby
made the fight hard on me already
I couldn't chase you anymore—for our son I had
to remain steady
I cried so much, and I prayed all the time
I couldn't believe to drugs I lost what was
rightfully mine
I begged you whenever you came home to get
some help
You claimed you could kick the habit by yourself if
you tried
You promised you would, and you wiped the tears
from my tired-eyes
But once I went to school you were at it again
You tried to do what was right
But to you the drugs were your only friends
I had to realize I lost the fight
I had to give up—the drugs had a grip on you too
tight
I left you
Subsequently, I regretted I did
We were apart three and a half years
Within those years I made choices I didn't want to
make
Took chances I didn't want to take
Sometimes I blamed it all on you
Because you didn't do what you were supposed to
I loved you, and you let me down
I wanted you to always be around

After almost four years we were together again
You had been clean for almost three years, and
you were the man you had once been
I came to Atlanta, and we went out on a couple of
dates
In less than a year you quit your jobs—moved
where I lived—so we could rekindle our fate
We were a family again
I felt really bad for your girlfriend
I didn't want to see the tears fall from her eyes
when she realized you were coming with me
You were always mine, and by my side you had to
be
A year later we were married again
Our son walked me down the aisle, and love
walked in
I was happy—thought this was it for my life
Thought this time you and I had it right
Why a year and six months later you cheated on
me
Made a mess of a good thing
And it was all for the sake of playing a game
Sometimes during my pain I wished I were
heartless as you
And for revenge be with someone else too
However, God blessed me with a conscience
To realize vengeance is nonsense
You asked me, and I told you that
After your affair I had feelings for a friend I
enjoyed talking to
But we never did what you and ol' girl would do
I never copulated with him
Although my hurt and temptations wanted to take
me there

I wished about your feelings I didn't care
Now you want to tell me how much you need me
But while you were intimate with her, who did
you need
Now you want to kill yourself if I'm not by your
side
Well, when she gave you fellatio did you try
No, killing yourself then wasn't in your plan
Because while you were cheating on me with her,
you thought you were the man
See, I know I am a good woman, and you had no
excuse
When you worked late at night, I worked hard too,
and I still waited up for you
You never had to come home to a dirty house
All you had to do was honor your spouse
But your sorry tail couldn't do that
Tore my life apart and now you want me back
How can I trust you; my mind will never rest
How am I supposed to give this mess my best
See, now you tell me how you were insecure and
really didn't think you could keep a woman like
me
Said you thought one day if I found better I would
leave
Well, I don't know how you thought that
If you were that insecure, after I left the first time
you should have never begged to come back
I stuck by you when we were young, and you went
to jail over two times
I stuck by you because you needed me by your side
Then even through your drug addiction I stayed
And like a good wife I got on my knees and for
"us" I prayed

Yes, I left when I couldn't take anymore
But it took me so long you didn't think I would
walk out the door
Then I gave you a second chance
Here we are today, and you still messed it up like a
dumb-man
Now when I talk about divorce you look away
Said you don't want to hear that word and want
me to stay
Well, I don't think I can be good to you
And I want to be a good wife and do the things a
wife should do
Sometimes I feel sorry for you
Because I know you have to be insecure to
sabotage yourself over and over again
Said if I forgive you, you will be a better husband
All you need is one more chance
Are you crazy; I won't put my heart back into your
hands

Dude, I gave you a second chance
See, I loved you so much I forgot you were just a
man
God brought me down to reality
Because I ran to him when you cheated on me
See, I loved you so much—sometimes
incognizant—I put you before God
God had to show me who would be there when
things got hard

This is truly my life story
To God I ask for forgiveness of my sins

Shay Seven

And to God I give the glory!

In hindsight, I was married very young because I did not have my father. I longed for my father, but he never treated me how I wanted to be treated. He gave me money when I went to his club, his TV repair shop, or his store. We talked a little—very little. I always caught the bus home. I can remember my father driving me home once. I resented my father for treating his kids by his wife better than he treated me. He had several businesses, and he and his wife had a home. I lived in the projects with my struggling single mother. We didn't even have a car. I was filled with anguish that was sometimes hard to articulate. As a child I did not understand the logistics of relationships. All I knew is that I wanted to be loved by my father.

I didn't receive that love, so early in life I tried to create that love. I married at sixteen years old. I always tried to do the right things although they often turned out wrong. My ex-husband and I loved each other, but there was so much to learn. He grew up in a group home. He still doesn't know who his father is today. And from what he recollects his mother never visited him in the group home, although she lived in the same city as he did. Hence I could never blame him for loving me the best way he knew how to love me while we were married.

The second time we were married I thought he had matured. He did in some ways, but some things had not healed in him. I thought we had it right the second time, but after his brief infidelity my ex-husband revealed to me how insecure he was in our marriage. I knew that he was being honest with me because I often felt his insecurity, but I thought my love would be enough. I don't think it was. We are divorced today, but we are great friends. We have our challenges, but we work through them because we love each other as family and friends.

20

I AM NOT ALONE

God, tell me what I am here to do
I know I was blessed from birth
You watch over me as I travel this journey on
earth
God, things have been arduous
I know you know
Sometimes I wonder how I stayed afloat
I am not perfect; yet, I have tried to live my life the
best I could
I have had several downfalls
They have been caused by my weakness to man
God, fornication is a sin is what I have been taught
So I have tried to be married all my life
Irrespective, I feel I have lost
I give all of me, and constantly I am hurt
Life isn't fair; how could I continue to feel like dirt
How can I continue to choose the wrong man
I am his wife, but still he doesn't understand
That I am his prize to be held high
Instead he stabs me in my back
And I have to watch him out of the side of my eye
God, all I want is love and happiness
I want to know with my husband I am blessed
And he'll be there for me
He'll treasure me because I am his destiny
When he hurts he will reach out to me, and I will
share his pain
When he is happy, I will share his gain
When someone does me wrong, he will stand up
for me
He'll go more than an extra mile if need be

His back will possess the bone that's needed to
ensure a woman like me
That I can sleep well at night because he will die
for his family
A man who looks at me and sees the depths of my
soul
I will be his queen even in the darkest of times
He will be my sun, and I will follow his sunshine
We will pray and grow together
He will never think about being without me ever
I won't crowd his space when he needs to be alone
to think
But he won't need much space because his heart
will crave for me with intensity
He will be my everything; I won't even glimpse at
another man
I will only praise and love my husband
Those things sound so good, and I know exactly
what I want
I have married men who think they know what
marriage takes, but really don't
I have stuck by them even in the darkest of times
On some occasions stuck by them so much, I must
admit I was blind
I have not been perfect God when they have
wronged me though
I have done things that could have buried my soul
I know although I feel betrayed I should continue
to live my life right
But when I think of how bad they did me and how
good I was, evil in my mind takes flight
I low rate myself by trying to get on their levels
When I should just keep doing right and arrest the
devil

God, please forgive me for the wrong things I have
done
Love me and help me to carry on
I feel like I'm always giving my all
And just when I feel secure I begin to fall
But I won't hold on to negative thoughts anymore
I won't hold on to any baggage
Instead, I will let my hands remain free
Love you God because no one loves me like you
love me
No one sees the beauty in me that you and I see
With my love for you I know I will always love
myself
And one day I will find the love of that blessed
someone else
God, I will not rush it
And while I am unmarried I will not fornicate
I will try hard not to make the same mistakes
God, as you know I need you
Because nowadays men want more
If they can't lie down with you, it's a proven fact
that they are out of the door
I also have temptations of my flesh
And they are hard to fight when I feel like a
woman in distress
God, all I'm doing is telling you the truth
Therefore, when the fight gets too hard hold me
tight
And close my eyes so I can rest on those lonely
sleepless nights
Let me walk with my back arched and my head
held high
Because of the security I have knowing that You
are by my side.

MS. TIEA
(The name of the actual participant has been changed)

I thank God for helping me to forgive you
Because if you would have seen this poem before
I wasn't so nice
Lyrically, I put your throat to a knife
A sharp one
With a gun
I could not continue to walk around like that
I had to command my peace back
That meant I had to forgive him and you too
The grace of God made it easy to do
I pray for you now
I pray that God has mercy on you
Because you plotted against my family
Took the very peace that kept me
But my husband left a crack in the door
When he should have made sure it was closed
tight
But he entertained your games
And became inflamed
With lust for you
It's okay—well it wasn't okay—but it's okay NOW
From the outset
I called you every name in the book
And when I finished that book
I made another book
Because you took
My peace
I came to your job
And cut you up with words as you sobbed
You ran into the bathroom stall
And I went around to every counter in the mall

A DIVERSIFIED BLACK WOMAN: I FEEL SO BLESSED

And told all your co-workers what you did
I was livid
You told me you knew Judo
And I told you to prove it
Because I knew Ghetto
It was crazy
And I am laughing now
But then
I wanted to check your chin
You hurt my family
And I wanted to hurt you
But God has always been in me
So I prayed for you
Because my husband made a choice to lay with
you
I didn't want you to ever feel what I felt
I didn't want you to feel like death
So I don't hate you—anymore
I walk in unconditional love
And I pray that God has mercy on you
Because you brought a curse to yourself
For intruding on my family
My husband belonged to me
And he was wrong
Right along
With you
And you both must pay
Because you stepped away from God's grace
For that ramifications are great
They have already been put in place
However, I wish no bad on either of you
In fact, my ex-husband and I are now great friends
Our marriage we couldn't mend

But today I pray that God continues to show you
mercy and gives you wisdom…
Mercy God—have mercy on her for me…

You have to pray good for your enemies. Sometimes it
is hard to pray for someone who has wronged you.
Therefore, pray for his or her salvation and for that person
to develop a true relationship with God. It is the easiest
way to pray for an enemy, and it is the greatest prayer to
pray for anyone. Irrespective of how mad you are with a
person, you should never want his or her soul to perish.
Sometimes when people do not act like God, it is because
they do not fully know him. In order for people to see their
wrong they have to see God clearly.

GOD'S PLAN

I wish I could take the world's pains away
I wish that people understood that we could make
the world a better place
If we tried hard to be good and have pure thoughts
We could rid the world of some of our faults
It's not the world that is evil or deceitful
It's the corrupt things we do and how we hurt
other people
If we took time to open our minds to the world's
natural beauty
It wouldn't be so hard to make taking care of the
world our duty
If we could only understand "God's Plan"
And the power that he has placed in our hands
Maybe then we won't be afraid to love each other
And look out for the well-being of our sister and
brother
But times show we don't understand
And with time evil is taking over man
Stop and take a look at what is going on
Don't let God's greatest creation be torn
If ever you question whether there is or is not a
God
Just think—what man could create the sun and
moon
What man could create the concept of birth
Breathe actual life on earth
Remember that there is a much higher power we
have to answer to
Remember that in "His plan" He unconditionally
loves you.

"It is incumbent upon us to take care of the gifts God has conferred on us—the earth and all in it."

"Money cheapens the value of life."

I'M SO TIRED GOD—I JUST WANT TO BE HAPPY

God, I'm just so disgusted with men
The minute you put them on a pedestal
Their unfaithfulness walks in
God, I truly ask you is there a man on earth who
can be true
Do as a husband what he has vowed to do
All I have ever wanted was someone to love me
unconditionally like I love them
Give me the devotion I give him
I know I deserve that in my life
I'm not saying I'm perfect, but if he tells me what's
wrong I will compromise
For the presence of true love there is nothing that I
wouldn't try
After all I have been through
My heart still aches for something warm and true
That special someone who needs love too
See, my smile has so many dimensions
So many dimensions I have people fooled
God, I don't know why I don't feel complete
I can't cry anymore; I'm all cried out
It's just so cloudy, and it's unbearably hard for me
to see
I really go crazy when I hear love songs that
describe my life
Sometimes the pain is so deep it cuts like a knife
God, I pray every night for you to show me which
road to take
Guide me and help me to concentrate
See, I'm trying to hold myself up like I know I have
to
Bear my pain and wait patiently on you

God, I just know I have got to be happy
But even when you show me which road to take
When I'm ready will there be a man for me
A man who first loves you
A man who is equal to me and takes his wedding
vows true
God, while I'm writing this poem tears come to my
eyes
Because living is so hard but I'm not ready to die
See, when your heart is broken it's like sugar-
drops in the rain
It's never really solid again
God, just get me through this tunnel that shows
very little sunlight
Help me find peace as you hold me tight.

In 1999 my father had cancer. I returned to Atlanta to help him. My family and I moved our furniture to Atlanta one week, and the next week we came to Atlanta permanently. After I returned to Atlanta, within three months I lost everything.

Since my family was moving abruptly, my father told me not to worry about living expenses in Atlanta. He disclosed to me that he had some money saved, and he would make sure we had a place to live. However, my father died the morning of my return. I lost my father, and my family didn't have a place to live. I was devastated. From that point on, my life experienced a downward spiral. My family and I went from living in a home in Hinesville to sleeping on the floor of a family member's apartment.

My husband cheated on me around the time of my father's death. I actually decided to divorce my husband because of the timing of his infidelity, and he lied about the details of his affair. I wanted to know all the details because the damage of infidelity had already been committed. My ex-husband thought lies would spare my feelings. But he didn't know that I was evaluating whether I should remain with him or not by his honesty. His mendacious character made me decide that our marriage was over.

Divorcing my ex-husband was one of the hardest things I had to do because I thought we would be together forever. It was our second time being married to each other, and we were a little older. I thought we had it right. But life is full of surprises. Satan can use everything against you if given a chance. You can be doing extremely well one day, and the next day everything you felt secure about can be taken away. I was very lost after my father's death and my husband's infidelity. Very depressed, there were times I felt my sanity evaded me. God really carried me during this time; I survived. However, it was not easy. I picked up some war scars along the way. The scars have healed, and I am a seasoned soldier today.

Now I know that my happiness is not contingent upon what is going on around me. True happiness is inside of me. Also my trials and tribulations have taught me the importance of not judging others. I have found that no matter how well we plan or how hard we work, we cannot control everything that happens in our lives. I am stern sometimes with what I believe, but I try hard to understand first and stifle judgment immediately. Being quick to judge is a sign of immaturity. If you live a little longer and allow life to show you its schematics, you will learn to be slow to speak about the problems and failures of others.

GOD

Something so deep inside of me
A spirit that sets my life free
More than any man could ever mean
More than any person could ever believe
Keeps me grounded when I feel faint
Keeps me focused when it's hard for me to think
Makes me believe in the things I can't see
Gives me unbelievable faith in my destiny
A feeling of presence when I reach out
A good feeling that makes me shout
Hope, determination, and pain
An experience that leads to internal and external
gain
Receives more uproar than any topic known
But with God's Spirit we will never be alone.

"No matter how we put the puzzles together, we need
God."

MY GRANDMOTHER

I must say she's quite a lady
Gave birth to ten
And they gave her over twenty-five grandchildren
Sensitive
Caring
Kind
Warm
A strong beautiful lady in her own right
Has come through the toughest of times and the
hardest fights
She'll give anything for the love of her kids
She's in my opinion one of the greatest women
who ever lived!

I wrote this poem for my grandmother while she was alive.

In late February of 2003, my mother had a brain
aneurysm. On March 8, 2003, on the way to visit my
mother at the hospital, my grandmother suffered a brain
aneurysm in the backseat of my stepfather's car. My baby
sat in his car seat to my left, and my grandmother sat to my
right. I was frantic. After a few tests, March 9, 2003, my
grandmother was declared brain-dead. I had a newborn
baby. My oldest son was in middle school; therefore, I had
to continue sending him to school. Moreover, I had to visit
my mother in the hospital and help plan my grandmother's
funeral. It was difficult, but with the grace of God I did
what was required of me. Although the doctors were not
sure my mother would survive, she survived. I had no time
to grieve for my grandmother until after she was buried. I
really miss my grandmother. She was one of the funniest
women I knew.

MY MOTHER

You have blessed me from birth
It didn't matter about the hard times we shared—
we had you
When our fathers were nowhere to be found, we
asked you why
You tried hard to explain to us
I was a little older, so I could see
That while you tried hard to explain it wasn't easy
I know you cried when we were not around
Because I could feel your tears when you looked at
me
So I tried hard not to make you unhappy
I saw some of the things you went through, and I
wished I could have taken them all away
Yet, I had faith that God would soon bring a
brighter day
I look up to you because of your strength
Your struggles do not make you a bad mother
In fact, they make you the best
Because you held on when you had worst
problems than the rest
So hold your head high because you played your
hand
You were the best mother, and today it still stands!

Dedicated to my mother Diane

GHETTO QUEEN

Your beautiful skin and your much needed smile
Your tender love and your unique style
Your pinto beans, neck bones, and cornbread
The way we all waited until you were asleep and
crowded into your bed
The way you said little things when you talked too
fast
Even the spankings you gave us when we were bad
The way it would storm and you would bring us in
your room so that we were all together
Knowing that with you things could not be any
better
You are our Ghetto Queen; you were all we had
There was no one else—no sight of our "ghetto
dads"
You gave us love and stuck by us like there was no
end
You were our Ghetto Queen, our Ghetto Dad, and
our Ghetto Friend
We were not rich, and I wouldn't have traded you
to be
Because you instilled things in us that are much
too deep
Nothing could ever replace that crazy laugh you
have
There could never be another
You are our Ghetto Queen, and we are your
struggles that prove there is nothing like a loving
mother!

Dedicated to my mother Diane

MY BROTHER

Oh how we would fight and raise so much hell
And in a brief moment all would be well
You wanted to be the oldest, but you were not
I was the oldest—a girl—and it made your temper
hot
Mad at the world because you were the only boy
Thought things should go your way and because of
Mom sometimes they did
But together my sister and I made you wish you
had never lived
We would make you see things would go our way
But we will always love you until our dying day!

Dedicated to my brother Willie

God has really spared my brother's life several times.
When he was perhaps about four years old, his nursery
blew up. His teacher saved him, and she returned inside to
rescue more children. There was a second explosion. His
teacher lost her life. My brother and mother were on the
front page of the AJC (Atlanta Journal Constitution) during
that time. When he was in the first grade I tried to wake
him up for school, and he didn't wake up. He shook
uncontrollably, and his eyes rolled back into his head. He
had a seizure that led him into a coma. He stayed in a
coma for two weeks. When he came out of the coma he
told us all how he saw God and Superman. Superman led
him away from the light. We were all amazed. As an adult
he was shot five times by someone who tried to rob him.
He really has survived a lot. However, I pray that he soon
recognizes all that God has brought him through and lives
his life solely for God.

MY GAY SISTER

It's incredible how things come to be
You were about three-feet-five
And now you're about five-feet-three
Long thick plats hung from your head
Now you choose a low textured fade instead
You never liked wearing dresses or any type of
girl-wear
You were a young girl I felt in despair
I could see you change, but I loved you so
And to me it was important to let you know
Soon you were just who you wanted to be
You are my gay sister, the youngest of three

Dedicated to my sister Shuntay

My sister is gay, and I don't judge or shun her. I have
told her what is in the Bible about homosexuality and
lesbianism. However, I respect and love her as my sister. I
let God's light shine through my life. I don't point my
finger at her every second of the day. I do not ram the
Gospel down her throat. I pray for her continuously, and I
trust that God will set her free. We have to allow God to do
for others what he has done for us, and it takes time. My
ex-husband and I had premarital sex. God had to set me
free from believing premarital sex was acceptable. God
understands the intricacies of his people because he created
us. Therefore, he knows what it will take to change lives.
As God's Apostles, we have to preach and teach the Gospel.
Moreover, allow God and the Gospel to transform people.
True transformation occurs from the inside-out, which
only God can do.

MY SON

When I found out about you, I had no idea what I
would do
Not because I didn't want you
But I didn't know how I would take care of you
I was eighteen and stressed
But it was heaven knowing with you I was blessed
Your father and I were young, but together we
would work things out
You had two parents who loved you without a
doubt
I would talk to you as you lie in my stomach and
call you by name
You had taken over and became my everything
When you were born your father cut the umbilical
cord
I was tired, and with a breath of air I gave thanks
to the lord
Your cries were like music to my ears
With time God healed all my fears
God promised to take care of me
He had given me a FAMILY
Not for me to be scared but to embrace
You are MY SON, A PRESENCE OF GOD'S GRACE!

Dedicated to my oldest baby, Bradley

MY SECOND BUNDLE OF JOY

My second bundle of joy
God blessed me with another wonderful baby boy
Your little hands
Your small feet
Your soft rosy cheeks
I have been blessed again
I look into your eyes
I comfort you when you cry
Nurture you from my breast
As you lie close to my chest
I put you beside me at night
Just to watch you sleep and hold you tight
I love the fact that you need me
Your love brings me glee
I smell your sweet breath
Smell and rub your hair
Kiss your poked-out lips
Imitate your bottom lip-dip
The completion of my heart
The answer to my prayers
God answered me!
He gave me you
As your mother, there is nothing for you I
wouldn't do.

Dedicated to my youngest baby, Jalen

KIDS RISE FROM THE GHETTO

GHETTO is just a WORD!
It never meant anything to me
Because I could dream
As long as I could see it
I knew I could do it
I had to empower me
And I couldn't allow the **"Poison"** into my skin,
which had taken my community
Other people who may have had a little more can
say what they want
But my dreams always gave me more than what I
could see physically
Walking out of my door with acts of desperation
surrounding me
But see ah, let go of my dreams and cave in—
never
My steps may take longer to climb, but with time
things will get better
Seize every chance I get
Fight with no regrets
Put all haters in check
Don't wait on anyone to hand you your piece of
the pie
If you can create a way, make a way for your
dreams to fly
Don't worry if your start is small or slow
Don't let your struggles make you let your dreams
go
Remember the story of the rabbit and the turtle's
race
The rabbit was fast in the beginning

A DIVERSIFIED BLACK WOMAN: I FEEL SO BLESSED

The turtle was slow, but he received all the
winnings
The turtle got to see all the sights
The rabbit saw no sights and lost the fight
If your friends have everything now—so what
Your start may be small, but if you keep pushing,
soon you will develop the Midas touch
With your slow start you gain wisdom and your
struggles build character
So don't let where you live take over you
Let it be **SPINACH** to your soul
Gain strength to fight and achieve your goals
Be who you are
Because you are truly a *shining-star*
Jesus said unto any person that believe, anything is
possible
So believe and don't give up
Although it gets tough
As long as you are alive you can overcome it
Fight like crazy—you can make it
Believe in you when no one else believes
See pass what's in front of you—have faith and
receive
And remember **"GHETTO"** has nothing to do with
you and your progress
So leave all negativity behind, and don't believe
that crazy mess
You can do it
Make it happen for you

When it's all over let your shine be the proof!

A WOMAN'S TEARS AND A GIRL'S FEARS

A GIRL'S TEARS AND A WOMAN'S FEARS

I watched my mother get beat to a pulp almost
every day
From one relationship to another
The more I prayed she would leave
The more she would find a reason to stay
I cried inside almost every night
I hurt for her
Although the sun shined, our days were seldom
bright
She jumped from windows
Ran out of doors
She tried hard to be the best
But every day life brought about unfamiliar tests
Stitches in her head
She lay sore in her bed
No man ever appreciated the woman she is
But I don't think she realizes how precious she is
Beautiful and so much to gain
But being abused caused her much pain
Times were hard, and I saw her cry
When I didn't see her tears I knew she tried hard
to hold them inside
She was all we knew, and we didn't want to lose
her
Sometimes on the way home from school I would
pray
God, please let my mother be okay
And if he does beat her, please let him wait until
we get home

So we can get her some help—don't let her face it
alone
We all cried
We couldn't sleep
Afraid of being awakened from the sounds of her
frightened feet
Although I tried not to fall asleep, soon my eyes
would get heavy
Once I felt sure it would be a peaceful night
Just as I got into my zone I would awaken from a
fight
No—fighting takes two
My mother was simply battered and abused
I couldn't rest
My siblings couldn't rest
All I can say is, thank God our mother is alive and
looking her best.

"We all have baggage. However, sometimes we are forced
to carry bags that are not ours, and they can take a lifetime
to understand and unload."

From what I recollect, my mother never fought back as
an abused woman. I would ask her why, and she told me it
would only make things worse. When I got older I
declared no man would hit me without remembering me. I
was very dominating in my marriages because of what I
watched my mother go through. I walked around ready
for a man to push my button so that I could challenge him.
However, God showed me the error of my ways. My
thinking was tainted by my childhood. A healthy
relationship between a man and a woman was never
modeled for me. God taught me what a healthy
relationship should exemplify.

Shay Seven

LOVE

Sometimes I wonder
Will I ever find that special man who believes in
love like I do
I don't understand why men feel they have to
cheat
It hurts the good wives
It destroys their lives
Sometimes you try to hold on, but it gets so hard
You become used to that other person because they
know you, and you know them
However, when they deceive you, the light that
shined so brightly becomes dim
You say it will be okay
But truth is it never is
You get to see another day
But it takes away a piece of you the more you try to
stay
It works for some, but it didn't work for me
I had to have **LOVE** for myself, so leaving was
PEACE.

"Sometimes we crave for love on the outside without loving
and understanding what is on "our" inside first."

I'M DIGGIN' YOU
First poem ever written for D'Wmac

I have never had a feeling like this about someone
new
It's indescribable because I'm diggin' you
I glanced at you because of your unique style
Every day you would pass by and smile
You never really said too much—quiet as can be
Even quiet with how you approached me
It was your smile, sexy walk, and quietness that
attracted me
Oh God, I have to shake this feeling I would say to
myself
But seeing you every day didn't help
It's not the right time
Maybe in another life it would be fine
When I talk to you I can't help myself
I'm straight-up diggin' you, and I have no idea
what's left
I just want to bask in your warm company
With that let whatever will be, be.

A WOMAN SHORT OF HER ROAR

(In reference to my husband)

Forgive me if your breakfast isn't hot like you like
it don't blame it on me—you woke up late
I washed the clothes and forgot a couple of your
special pieces
Next time put them where I can see them
I was late picking you up today
I was tired; I fell asleep
I have a can in the car, and you just cleaned it the
other day
What about your shoes in the floor after I cleaned
the house
I didn't have dinner ready, and I have been home
all day
You have two hands God gave you
I fell asleep while you were telling me about your
day at work
You picked the wrong time

(In reference to my son)

I got you to school late, and you had to go straight
to class
Well, you ate breakfast at home anyway
I picked out some pants that fitted a little too well,
and your friends laughed at you all day
Mommy really sorry baby
In front of the school, I licked my hand and wiped
your face in front of your friends
Then poked my lips out for you to give me a kiss

A DIVERSIFIED BLACK WOMAN: I FEEL SO BLESSED

Well, you kiss me all the time at home with no
problem
I forgot to go to the grocery store and get your
favorite foods with the cartoons on the boxes
Child, eat something else without the illustration

I am tired; did anybody hear me!
I am not perfect!
I know that you guys think that I can do
everything and so much more.
But today this loving wife and mother is A
WOMAN SHORT OF HER ROAR!

HAPPINESS

Tired of the lonely tears that fall from my eyes
The salty tears that soak my face
I am trapped in my own mind
I can't figure out how to get out of this place
I try so hard, but I can't find freedom
I look around and see things I think will make me
whole
I can't grasp them
I try to be patient, but I have no room
I am suffocating
I have journeys that I want to take
But with bars surrounding me where can I go
How can I be rescued?
When I think I have the key
It never sets me free
Am I a fool because of the lonely tears I cry
Am I a fool to keep on trying
Am I a fool to keep on praying
Am I a fool to believe I will take those journeys I
long to take
Will I ever be free
Will I ever be HAPPY?

"Is happiness what we think it is? Or is happiness a word
to define an illusion?"

MY GREATEST FEAR

God, I look around and sometimes I am confused
I feel lost, and I am afraid to lose
God, my greatest fear—I know you know
Is to die without being successful
I have got to have more than a taste of it
I can't leave this world without making it
I have a lot of talent and so many dreams
I am innately business savvy
But no one on my team
At least no one who can show me the ropes
But as long as I have your "Spirit" I know there is
hope
I have to make a difference in this world, and that
is all I see
I want to be a master at whatever I do
If I don't, I know my soul will forever bleed
See God, no one knows how my veins ache for
success
Unattained goals are the cause of my unhappiness
I try so hard, and I know if I had more time,
money, and people with connections to contact
Success would be mine at the drop of a hat
I have hope that it is right around the corner
I have to remain patient and wait
Because I know what I am going through to get
there is going to make sure I appreciate
All the blessings right now that only you and I can
see
In fact, sometimes I am so caught up in the
moment I don't realize
I have the **"World's Greatest Contact"** by my side
So every day I work a little harder and hold on

Because I know that with God, success will not be
long.

"Success is not always tangible."

"Rejection is not the end of the world; it is the beginning of
a business plan and opportunities unknown."

BABY

When I look into your sweet innocent eyes
And feel the softness of your skin
I think to myself, this is where it all begins
Hold your tiny hands up to mine
Kiss your cute little lips while you are asleep
This is the best thing that ever happened to me
The smell of your breath
Or the way you suck on your hands
Your fat little legs
Your silky hair
I know this wonderful feeling is beyond compare
Feeding you from my breast
As I hold you close to my chest
It's the greatest feeling in the world to know that I
have given life
And I have what it takes to nurture you to grow
This is one time I know
That I am surely a **REMARKABLE WOMAN**

Dedicated to my boys

I have heard the saying "a woman cannot raise a man." I strongly disagree. If you are blessed to have a good man as the leader of your household, you should thank God for that man. However, if you are a single mother raising your son, you must work harder to make your son understand why it is important to be a wonderful man. I love teaching my sons how to treat women—open doors and pull out chairs—who better to teach them than me. I am not trying to make the fathers obsolete. We need them if they desire to be around. However, if they do not want to be around, their absences should not hinder the rearing of our children. We cannot appease ourselves with excuses. We have to do what we have to do as loving mothers. Some things will go wrong, but if you apply yourself, you have a better chance of them going right. Some men grew up in two-parent households, but their fathers never did anything with them. Therefore, it was as if single mothers reared them.

Society classifies families led by single mothers as dysfunctional families. Dysfunctional means something is not functioning properly. My kids and I function with love every day. There is nothing dysfunctional about that. I will not allow people to place that title on my family because we do not have a man as the head of our household. No offense intended men, but women, sometimes the men we have in our lives put the "dys" in dysfunctional. A man is not tantamount to "function." What disturbs me is that a single man with kids is never labeled as having a dysfunctional family. He is highly esteemed for taking on a job he wouldn't normally face alone. Yet, the families of single mothers are emasculated daily.

When you allow people to define you and your family, you will subliminally embody their definition. Do not allow others to impose their definitions on you. Define your family yourself. My family is God and love. It wasn't my plan to be alone raising my boys. However, I am not going to allow people to tell me because I am a woman I cannot fully raise my sons, especially when I do the job every day with passion and energy. Moreover, I know that I can do all things with God who gives me wisdom. Therefore, women take pride in rearing and teaching your sons to be wonderful men. Don't half-do the job because you are single. Work harder and smarter (call on God). The last time I checked being single was not a handicap but a marital status.

2PAC

When I first heard your voice it was deeper than
just a rap to me
In so many ways, I could feel your soul
In so many ways, I felt there was more to you than
anyone could see
The first hard-core rap artist I ever took to
Your praising of women—how you told them to
keep their heads up—made me want to meet you
I watched you on the news when you were in
trouble
Oh how I prayed for you, hoping you would see
the light
Hear your own words and figure out answers to
your own plight
You were a blessed individual, one of God's
greatest creations
A voice that played on every radio station
Sold more records than any rapper
Made other rappers see money could be made
And how in time they could live life in the shade
You didn't stop there, you continued climbing high
Doing movies, making double-tapes, and looking
"So Fly"
With age you got better
In "California Love" you looked so good in black
leather
You looked even better without a shirt
You looked so good—you made my eyes hurt
When I looked into your eyes
I understood you because I knew you rapped from
your soul

Like a musical poet going to work, you took
control
Although I never met you, I felt like I knew you
well
I was your number-one fan—faithful as you can
tell
The worst day in the entertainment world was
when I heard for the second time you had been
shot
I was like a worried wife or mother praying once
again God would pull you out
But I saw the words go across the TV screen
I couldn't understand it—how could life be so
mean
Just like you wanted to be when you died, you are
a "legend" to all
Like we all must do, you had to answer death's call
I just can't believe at 25 years-old your life was
copped
**You were the secret love of my life, THE WORLD'S
GREATEST 2PAC!**

This was written before I became a minister.
Irrespective of who I am, I respect the talent Tupac Shakur
possessed in his lifetime. He was beyond talented, and I do
not apologize for admiring his unbelievable ambition and
artistry. I believe he was a prophet that over a course of
time was deluded by Satan. I could not exclude this poem
from my book.

BB

The sweetest little girl I had ever seen
There was nothing in her body that was mean
Smart, beautiful, and special to me
A halo over her head that no one could see
God blessed her at birth
She had such a brief visit on earth
She was called home to God at the age of four
She was my little **BB**—the girl I adored!

In memory of my sweet Bianca

Bianca was my first cousin. I treated her like my daughter. I wasn't an average teenager. Most teenagers would rush off the school bus to be with their friends or to hang outside. I would do my homework and afterwards go get Bianca. I loved being a mother even before I biologically became one. My aunt had five kids that I would keep from time to time. However, I always kept Bianca. Sometimes I felt guilty for showing a difference, but it was just something special about her. I gave Bianca her middle name and nickname; I potty-trained her; and I got her ears pierced. Whenever I saw something that reminded me of her, I bought it. She was very special to me. Bianca passed away of AIDS.

THE GUNSHOT

He was young
And like anyone he made a couple of mistakes
But nothing egregious that he should have paid so
great
He was like a brother to me
We were two sisters' children
He was my family
I cried like a baby with colic
His life was taken with one click
Not lawfully a man yet
It was the gunshot that took my cousin's life and a
phone call I will never forget
I pray with the angels he reign
My heart aches because I lost my cousin James.

In memory of "Pnut"

My cousin James and I were the two oldest
grandchildren on my mother's side. I am the older of the
two. We were very close. He often referred to me as his
sister. When we got older, my cousin and I had several
conversations about making a difference in our family. I
wanted to see us succeed. He had just fathered a child.

My husband was in the military, and when Pnut was
killed I was away from home. I received a notification to
call home from the Red Cross. My husband answered our
phone, and he passed it to me. We had been playing before
the phone call, but after the call my husband's demeanor
changed. He was quiet, and he watched me intensely as I
called home. In hindsight, he knew something was wrong
because the Red Cross would only contact a person for

something important. When I called home my sister blurted out, "Pnut is dead!" I was so incognizant that I asked, "What Pnut?" We knew other Pnuts in the neighborhood. "Our Pnut!" Then she let out a loud cry. "No, no, no! He was going to go to Job Corp! He promised me he was going to do something with his life! Noooo!" I screamed. My husband held me in his arms and rocked me. He called his sergeant to inform him of our situation. My husband immediately packed us up.

I was only three and a half hours away from Atlanta. When I arrived home, I went to my aunt's (Pnut's mother) apartment where I found my youngest aunt Trina crying and in disbelief as she swept her nephew's blood away. When she saw me she ran to me. We cried and held on to each other for a long time. I was told a bullet intended for someone else killed him. However, we know bullets do not have names. The story is so hard to tell because as I type about it, I relive it. It hurts. My youngest son crowded my space and asked me, "Mama, why are you crying?" His mother crying while typing on the computer probably seemed crazy to him. I had to tell him about his cousin he never knew. After hearing some of the facts my baby precociously said, "Mama, don't cry. You will see him again."

Pnut was only seventeen—a few months away from turning eighteen. His daughter only hears stories of her father because she was just a baby when he was killed. She didn't deserve to grow up fatherless. My cousin had a family that loved him, and his life was taken because of stupidity. He had dreams too. He had things that he wanted to accomplish and do. Yet, foolishness stole my cousin's fate. When the bullet leaves the chamber it's too late.

> I don't want to see another young person lose his or her life over a frivolous mistake. Life is too great!

57

THE HEAT THAT MELTED MY AUNT AWAY

She was heartless at times and strong as an ox
Ruthless, bold, and smart as a fox
She made the men wild and act insane
The women disliked her and called her out of her
name
She was beautiful with much pizzazz
But no one predicted what would happen down
her path
She went to the doctor early one day
Only to hear the horrible truth he would say
Subsequently, she lived her life depressed
She was in denial, and her life was a mess
She passed her unhappiness around from man to
man
Giving them what they thought they wanted and
all they could stand
Evil she did, but it gave her energy
But soon she couldn't take anymore—she was
much too weak
Unhappy and afraid she lived the rest of her life
She was not beautiful anymore, and she had lost
her fight
She was six feet under but out of pain
A disease that took her away with such a short
name
Never will the ones who loved her forget how
special she was
Praying that she rests with God up above.
In memory of Trina

Trina was Bianca's (BB) mother.

THE DEATH OF MY FATHER

I never really knew the actual man that you were
Although I dreamt of us being much more
There were many gaps in our relationship
In fact, I had given up—it was a part of life I
missed
Whoever knew you would need me
Whoever knew by your bedside I would be
I never wanted it to take an illness to draw us
together
I wouldn't wish or cause you any harm ever
But your illness was the cause of me getting closer
to you
We became father and daughter—something that
was overdue
You were an angel God resurfaced into my life
Answers to my buried plights
I desired more time
But I am thankful for the memories that are
forever mine
I love you father, and with God you now roam
God has made heaven your home.

In memory of Donald aka Honkey

WHAT DO YOU MEAN I AIN'T KEEPING IT REAL

Yeah, I came up in the hood
And it's still all good
But just because I moved out and want to have
things
Don't come tell me how I have changed
Nothing in life ever stays the same
I'm real as the next person
I know where I come from
Honey, the world is a huge pie, and I want some
I cannot help that you want to die in the hood **"still
keeping it real"**
Let me die leaving much money to my sons in
Beverly Hills
I am going to **"keep it real"** by doing well for
myself and helping others come up
It's about time we stop being stuck
That's **"keeping it real"** to me
If your **"keeping it real"** isn't the same as mine
Then you **"keep it real"** while you stay in the hood
While I **"keep it real"** inside!

"I will talk candidly about where I come from if you can
handle where I am going."

MY BROKEN HEART

The one I loved unselfishly
Whoever knew that you would betray me
You lived a secret life; Tiea was her name
You hurt me badly; it almost drove me insane
I would have done anything for you—even given
my life
I would have done what I had to because I was
your wife
It only took a split second for you to hurt me and
break my heart
I remember it so well; I cried all night in the dark
Love me you say but how could it be
You ran to her and depleted me
For the sake of playing a game you ruined your
family
With your eyes opened wide you still could not see
My veins hurt, and my heart pumped slow
You hurt me more than you will ever know
I couldn't work; you took my strength away from
me
It was the hardest experience in my life
It knocked me to my knees
I felt I had nowhere to turn and no one to talk to
My sun was gone, and my skies were blue
I called on God to help me make it, so I could be
strong for our son
With God's grace let his work be done
I knew God would not put anything on me that I
couldn't handle
In my darkness, God was the huge flame on my
tiny candle

That kept me going strong in order to find myself
again
God was my inspiration; he was the only one I
would allow in
Slowly but surely I came back
I forgave you for your other life and got mine back
on track
I gained my strength back, but what should I do
I chose to let you back into my life and love you
And about that I was confused
It was hard, and I knew it would never be easy
You did the unspeakable—you deceived me
You broke my trust and put out our flame
Although you have another chance, things will
never be the same
A lot of people may think I am insane for forgiving
you
They don't know the other loving things you do
My forgiving you is true love to me
And together I want our family to be
I prayed that you deserve your chance
And now you know what it means to be a devoted
husband!

"Someone once said that to forgive is to forget. I tell you
it's not true. For example, many African Americans have
forgiven the white race for their cruel treatment to them in
the past. However, it is hard not to remember the facts.
Forgiveness simply takes away the 'hate' from
remembering."

THE TUNNEL THROUGH HER EYES

I can remember the day I received the call
After all my tears I cried, all I could think about
was you
I knew James was your life, and for your kids there
was nothing you wouldn't do
You loved them the best way you knew how
You were a good mother, and that was without a
doubt
I can remember walking into Punkin's house and
seeing your eyes
They were a tunnel to the hurt and full of the tears
you cried
I never want to know how it feels to lose a son
I was amazed at how you managed to carry on
I know burying your "Pnut" was not easy for you
But like always you stood up and did what you had
to do
I pray that someday God will help us all
understand
And don't worry—you are a wonderful mother
who raised your four boys to be men!

Dedicated to Carrie aka Sister

NOT ALONE

I am a woman who is sometimes as strong as a
man
But a woman who sometimes needs the touch of a
loving-hand
I have a career; I can pay my bills on my own
However, my heart aches at the thought of being
alone
I can run a business and handle life's stress
But I sometimes need a man's head to lie softly
against my breast
I can be celibate if I wanted to
But I rather make love to my husband near an
ocean-view
I can climb a mountain and cross a sea
Yet, I rather stay home with my husband and let
him sooth me
For all you "New Age" women who don't need a
man
You are by yourselves because I don't understand
If love is crazy, I'm insane
Because being alone is not my thang!

I never wanted to be alone. Yet the very thing I feared
was the best thing that could have ever happened to me. I
became acquainted with God and myself during my alone
time. I listened to God tell me about my mistakes, and God
and I worked on me. I have been divorced over ten years
now and celibate seven years. I want to get married again.
I love marriage. However, I know who I am now, which
makes God and me particular about the man who is placed
on the throne as my husband.

THE LOVE OF MY FATHER

Father, when I was young I craved for your love
I sometimes cried and asked God up above
Why you didn't love me
Why spending time with me was not where you
wanted to be
You gave me money and said a few sentences; that
was it
I wanted more than those little visits
See, I needed to be loved by you
I needed you to tell me you loved me too
I cried to my mother a few times
She was hurt too, so I wiped the tears from my
eyes
She had so much to deal with; therefore, she really
couldn't relate
She had far too much on her plate
No matter how I said it, she just did not
understand
Her logic was I had her—a girl didn't need a man
Father, I tried hard to tell you how I felt
I tried so hard, but my heart you would melt
I grew up a little fast, and I vowed to give my child
a family
A father and a mother who were married
When I did get a family, I tried hard to hold it
together
I went through a lot, but now I know better
I am a woman tougher than leather
Yet, as a woman I hurt for your love
I cried some nights because I felt I was the only
one who tried
Sometimes I didn't bother to come your way

Because I knew we would never have much to say
God knows it broke my heart
God knows it tore my world apart
I had to go on with my life because now I had a
son
I had to give him love and carry on
But about my broken relationship with you—I
cried
It hurt to know we were not even aware if one
another were alive
I gave you my number several times
But I was always calling you
This made me feel unloved and blue
I declared I wasn't calling anymore
Three years passed by, and we had not spoke
I knew that if I didn't call you, you would never
call me
You never had in my life
Made me feel like our relationship wasn't worth
the try
But later I got a call that would change my world
My father was ill, and I ran to you like a little girl
I was there for you; I was right by your side
Because I don't hold hate in my heart
I loved you so much that I ran at the chance of a
new start
You had cancer, and you didn't look the same
You were my father, and that would never change
You wanted me to move to Atlanta so that you
could live with me
See, for the love of my father I proved I would do
anything
I saw you get sicker, but I guess I was in denial

A DIVERSIFIED BLACK WOMAN: I FEEL SO BLESSED

I was so happy when I walked into your hospital
room and saw you smile
You made my days so bright
All I thought about was how I was going to get you
a little refrigerator for your room—while I worked
things would be in your reach
How I would get my mother to come over to
prepare you food to eat
I was like a little girl again
You brought me joy
When I finally came to Atlanta on February 5,
1999
In her driveway, my mother met me with news
that showed me again life wasn't always kind
You passed away on the same morning we came to
Atlanta to stay
I tried not to let hurt and sadness cover my face
I hurt badly, and I was angry because I thought I
finally had you
I felt so cheated once again
But I knew God had you in his plans
Now I am thankful for the memories that God gave
me of you as a token
Those memories helped heal a heart that for a long
time had been broken

I don't know why I did not realize my father was dying. I think
I wanted to be with him so badly that I was in denial. I had to
be in denial because everyone around me knew he was dying. I
was the only person shocked! If I knew my father was dying I
would have visited him as often as possible, but I wouldn't have
moved back to Atlanta at that time. In hindsight, I believe God
gave me closure with my father and memories of my father
while realigning me for my destiny in Atlanta.

LET THE ANGELS REJOICE

Angels fly
Although sometimes it's hard
We must say goodbye

You touched our lives tremendously
Although we hurt
We know heaven is where you were meant to be

Angels fly
So we know you have flown
You have your wings now
And you call heaven your home
Angels Fly...

**In memory of Yvonne
This poem was placed on her obituary.
I was her "Shalucy."**

...WHO IS THE THIEF?

Now is the future
But the past...
The past is the past
But when I see movies made which bring the past
to the future it makes me sad
It makes me mad!
The way black people were treated was evil and
insane
The way we were railroaded causes me pain
Pain to my heart
Some of the things that were done to us I couldn't
have done to a stray dog
Were the people doing it of God?
I mean, that is my question
I don't understand it
Sometimes it hurts so deep
Because I thought as long as I had love and
believed
Life would be okay
But why wasn't it okay for them?
Why did our people have to suffer?
And some suffered to their end
Innocent human beings
Human beings—you hear me!
It is not the point of black and white to me
To me it will never be
But what about flesh and blood
They were people
Made in God's image too
It doesn't matter whether they were black or blue
They had a heart, a spirit, and a soul
But still they were victims of cold

Shay Seven

Cold that is sometimes intolerable to see acted out
in a movie
I can't!
So many questions run through my mind
I know God is just
But I wonder why our ancestors had to suffer for
us
Why couldn't we just be?
Why so much tragedy had to cloud our history?
Why were we called niggers?
To make the so-called intelligent white man feel a
little bigger
Always trying to define us and how we feel
Your need to control kills
In sixty-five you murdered our X
Because he didn't mince his words or take your
mess
I don't care what the history books speculate
I believe the white race stole his fate
In sixty-eight you dethroned our King
Thinking it was going to kill "his dream"
But it didn't
One seed sprouts up a massive harvest
We still know his name
And the vision that God gave him continues to
reign
Although you try very hard to bury it
Something you will never admit
He has a day to celebrate his legacy
Memorials up everywhere
Even in Washington D.C.
Where black people and righteous white people
gathered to hear his dream
He lives, and his voice continues to sing

"Free at last! Free at last! Thank God Almighty we
are free at last!"[2]
I know it's not good to question God
But I wonder why things had to be so unfair and
devastatingly hard
For my people
Some white people hold their heads so high
As if they have done everything right
Lived a dignified life
You walk around proud of your history and tell us
we should be ashamed of ours
WHAT THE HELL ARE YOU SO PROUD OF
Your ability to encapsulate Satan and his
infiltrating ways so well
Your ability to manipulate and twist anything
Or maybe you're proud of how you are a control
fiend
No, no, I know what it is—don't tell me
It's how you turned kings and queens into slaves
Whom your capitalization and cruel treatment
took to their graves
Maybe it's how you pimped your slaves to have
babies
Mated us like we were dogs and cats
You raped your slave women every day
Your wife didn't say anything because you had her
trained to look away
Your slave walking around with a blue-eyed baby
When her husband was blue-black
Her husband felt less than a man

---

[2] Dr. Martin Luther King, Jr. "I Have a Dream" speech was delivered at
the Lincoln Memorial in Washington D.C., August 28, 1963.

Because every night his wife had to give in to your
sexual demands
And the poor man couldn't do anything but watch
it happen
Or die trying to stop you
He already worked feverishly for you
And you still had to take the little that he had
I got to give it to you, when you want to kill a
person you make sure they are dead
AND YOU CALL US ANIMALS
You specialized in dehumanizing us
Your barbarian ways **DISGUST ME!**
You really have something to be proud of

I WOULD CRY IF I HAD YOUR HISTORY
Because being a slave is better than **being a
product of Satan**
**God made you, but you cannot convince me that
Satan did not have your minds**
God did not condone how you treated us
And some of you continue to be indifferent, evil,
and deceitful
Point and jeer at my people
Call us the dregs of society
I think the ones that killed my people are the dregs
of society
Give me your logic about this, how can you cry for
Jesus
He is my Savior too, but how can you cry for
someone who was killed over 2000 years ago
Yet, you killed someone made in his likeness every
day
How can you find so much love in your heart for
God

But you clawed his Black people apart
And really you continue to do it today
In your covert ways
Please explain this to me
Because a true-lover-of-Christ will not see
What you did to my people as "right"
I question your love for Christ
And if you have not repented, you cannot
understand his life
You are so wise
In your own eyes
Say we are not educated like you
That makes you feel better about the crap you do
Remember that is how this thing all started
Those dumb archaic Africans needed you
Is how you legitimated your wrong
Yeah right, we needed you to put your feet on our
necks
We needed you to can us like sardines on a ship
Take us on a long life-threatening trip
Many of us died
Lonely and afraid
Some had to lie next to a dead body for days
You raped our women on those ships
You were so evil you probably raped some of our
men too
I don't put anything pass you
It is mindboggling how you viewed us as animals
that were not equal to you
But when you needed to put your penises in a hole
Our vaginas would do
Tyrants!

You are so smart let you tell it

But everything you have you exploited my people
to get
This country was built on my people's backs
Today you changing the stats like all of us populate
the welfare-line
When your people are there just like mine
This society kills and imprisons our men
Sometimes without giving them a fair chance
Skew the stats like we all have AIDS
As if all your people are disease-free, holy, and
saved
They have AIDS too!

You look at us like we stink
Your history is stinking up the entire nation!
God's nostrils burn at your past
The bodies you have wrongly killed are in heaven
waiting for you
The day is going to come where you get your due
You better make it right
Or it will forever be wrong
Repent before you go home
And repentance means admitting to your truth
Your veracity is your people were egregious to my
people
You killed us and failed to treat us equal
You have always tried to make us feel like we were
short of something
When you were always deficient
If you were not, you wouldn't have needed us
And every day you treat us like we are stealing
something
Pull your purse or bag closer to you when we
come around

Treat us like we are all lowdown
WHEN ALL YOU HAVE DONE IS STOLE
I am not prejudice
But the truth must be told

You stole our bodies
YOU STOLE OUR MEN
You stole our children
You stole our kin

You stole our sight
You stole our minds
You stole our freedom
You stole our time

You stole our sex
You stole our fight
You stole our dignity
You stole our might

You stole our sperm
You stole our traditions
You stole our milk
You stole our visions

You stole our inventions
You stole our peace
You stole our memories
You stole our grief

You stole our history
You stole our health
You stole our music
YOU STOLE OUR WEALTH

Shay Seven

NOW YOU TELL ME WHO THE HELL IS THE THIEF!

"We must all repent for our wrong. If we do not repent, we will answer to God. I am not prejudice, but I cannot deny the pain of my people to appease others. I love humankind, and I love the truth. If you have repented— which encompasses turning away from past behaviors—do not allow anyone to condemn you about your past."

SO I FELL

I felt so ashamed
Because I had actually lost my strength when I
experienced so much pain
My eyes were wide-opened, but I could not see
There was no one reaching out to help me
And so I fell
I fell to my knees
I was alone—at times afraid to try to look around
Had no idea how to break free
And so I fell
This time I almost lost my mind
I tried to smile, but it was fake
Put together from some of the fragments happiness
would dissipate
So my smile easily went away
Because it had no solid foundation to stay
And so I fell again
Somehow my eyes became uncovered; I could see
And this time when I reached out, there was a
hand without a face reaching out to me
It had been there all the time
It would pull me up and wipe away the tears I
cried
The darkness that shielded my eyes was my lack of
faith
Once I gained my faith, I could see the hand that
helped me rise and climb out of my lonely space
Although I fell and fell again
I reached out and took hold of the hand
There were times my hand was too weak to lift or
reach out

That's when the Spirit that beheld the hand came
down
I was so weak and tired from all my falls
About to give up on it all
But the Spirit would not let me give in
And each time I fell, the hand was there again and
again
I grew unafraid, and God taught me a love that
would no longer let me fall
I had faith that helped me through it all
Each test I passed, I grew a little more
Understanding what the hand was there for
It helped me gain wisdom and endure my tests
And gave me a KINGDOM MINDSET!

"You learn a lot when you fall. If you never fall, you won't
experience the power of getting up."

"The lesson is in the fall. The reward is in getting up."

MY BLACK QUEEN

To My Black Queen
Whom I highly esteem
Mother, I can't tell you enough how much I love
you
I appreciate the things you have done for me and
still do
Lady, you are amazing and to think about the
things you went through for us make me cry
But your struggles make me try
Mother, I was young and just thought you were
doing what you were supposed to
I never realized you struggled because of the love
you possessed for us inside of you
You could have aborted us or left us on the streets
But you didn't, and for you I want to be all I can be
See, it is okay now mother because your children
are grown
It's time for you to rest your feet and tired mind—
let us buy your dream-home
You know as long as I have it, it's yours
There will be nothing you will have to work for
Because you are quite a lady baby
I'm grown now, and I see how difficult it is
I see it takes God, hard work, faith, and strength to
live
The struggle is real
And it's funny how trials and tribulations can
make you feel
Mother, I have one child and a husband, and you
have three kids you raised by yourself
Therefore, I can only try to imagine how you felt
You strengthen me more than you will ever know

I am proud of you; I feel like I am the mother now
It's amazing how being an adult can make you see
That a parent's struggle isn't easy
Mother, I am so happy I had you
For me you did all that you knew to do
I raise you up because you are truly my BLACK
QUEEN
I raise you up because for your kids you would do
anything
That's a BLACK QUEEN if I have ever heard of one
A BLACK QUEEN who stands tall in the **rain** just as
she does in the **sun!**

Dedicated to my mother Diane

"A mother is there for the good times and the bad times."

BAD AS I WANT TO BE

God, I'm free
Free in my mind
Have the chains that once cut into my skin off of
me
I don't hear what anyone is saying
I'm living every day as if it's my last and constantly
praying
I know I am ready to live; I am not ready to die
I am hard as steel and ready to fight
It's time for me to shine, and I don't care what
people say
I'm taking over my destiny and clearing my
pathway
Of all the negative rubbish that tries to trip me and
make me fall
I have on my protective gear, and I'm ready to ball
I am crossing out everyone who is not truly for me
It's cold, but it's the way things have to be
I can see through the sheep's clothing
I am elevating and doing things God has told me
I am stronger now than I have ever been
I'm one person but inside strong as ten
A young woman who isn't afraid to look back
Because I'm not ashamed of my past now that I
have my life on track
I am not mincing what I have to say
If it bothers you please get out of my way
Devil, don't come on my stumping~grounds
GOD AND I WILL TAKE YOU DOWN

I have grown, and I know there is more for me to
see
Please get out of my way
Because I'm <u>BAD AS I WANT TO BE!</u>

"The devil can only do what you allow him to do. We have
to relinquish power for him to take power. Satan likes to
deceive us into believing that he has more power than we
do. However, Jesus freed us, and we are one with him.
Hence, our power transcends Satan's actions against us."

MY BABY EVEN WHEN YOU'RE 80

For you I will do anything
For you my heart sings
I will lay my life down for you
I will work my fingers to the bone if that's what I
have to do
You know you mean a great deal to me
Because Mama doesn't get her hands dirty for
anybody
I love my baby
You are a gift God gave me
The greatest gift I have received
If there is one thing I feel I have done great
It is giving birth to you and believing in fate
You are Mama's greatest joy
I will love you as a man the way I have loved you
as a boy
I try my best to teach you respect and to know and
call on God
Call on him before things get hard
Be a "Great" man baby—don't settle for good
Don't leave this world knowing that you didn't
give life all you could
Reach pass the stars
Reach baby!
Because you can be anything you want to be
I don't care what other people tell you!
You possess strength in you to do what God has
called you to do
I want you to be "Great" and choose a wonderful
woman whom you will love and appreciate
Raise your woman up like the Queen she is

Don't be intimidated by her being strong and hard
as steel
Let her shine too
Let her shine complement you
Be honest baby—treat people great
Do not view people solely by their mistakes
Be as close to perfect as you can
Be a strong, hard, successful, Godly man
Because to me you will always be Mama's baby
Mama's baby even when you're 80!

Dedicated to Bradley and Jalen

My kids are everything to me. God used them during difficult times to contain my sanity. There was a time I contemplated suicide, but I could never hurt myself after looking into their eyes. I wouldn't trade them for the world. When I answered my call as a minister, initially I did it for my kids. I realized no matter how hard I worked, I wasn't getting anywhere—at least not where I wanted to be. Spiritually, my family was cursed. I had to sacrifice myself to bring my kids and me out of those curses. It has been a very arduous and daunting experience. However, I know God's promises are true, and he will do what he said he will do. God's plan is not easy because it prunes me. Yet, I am a better person today because of God's pruning. I am more sympathetic and empathetic to others. I am more receiving, loving, and giving.

ANGEL

Angel, I am very proud of you
Because you finished school
See, now you have just begun
It was not easy—you experienced times where you
wanted to run
Do you know how many in our family in the
generation that you are in did what you have did
Pat yourself on the back because you are it
I want you to be all that you can be
Because you can—as long as you trust in God and
believe
If I get rich before you go to college
I don't want you to worry about money—just get
knowledge
I love to see people excel
But I don't put them down when they fail
I know if your mother were living she would have
been so proud of you going that mile
Angel, I wrote this from my heart
Because you now have in life one of the best starts
Keep pushing, dreaming, and achieving
When times get hard never stop believing.

Congratulations!

We had others to come after Angel. Congratulations to
Eric, Tricia, and Bradley. There will be many more!

20+

Girl, sometimes you can walk around in denial
With so many troubles—sad behind your beautiful
smile
I know because I always stayed in a size six
Weighing no more than 125—working it
Girl, I gained so much weight within a year and
six months
Looking as if I had eaten a cow for lunch
The sad part about it, I was walking around like I
was still fine
Lugging a tub of lard on my behind
Stuffing body parts in places they couldn't fit
And when people who love you look at you
They are in denial too
Because to them they love you any way you come
And to them you really are beautiful
They are not just turning on charm
But when those problems you have are over and
you can see
You see just actually what is happening
Honey, I looked like a quarterback
I couldn't believe I had allowed myself to get like
that
My waistline wasn't anymore
I realized I was looking fat in those little clothes
So I picked up my shoulders and decided to make a
change
Decided I didn't want to be overweight and
ashamed
I wanted to wear my little clothes again
I did what was right for Shay
And in me I trust

I felt like an iron pipe that couldn't be bent when I lost 20+!

I gained twenty pounds during the time of my divorce and period of depression. I actually like being curvy, but curvy for my body type doesn't exist without having a stomach. Where some women would have what we call a "muffin-top" (stomach fat spilling over their jeans) I would have an entire "cake." I have never been successfully curvy (thick according to some African Americans). Hence, I look better small. When I am small I still have some curves. I guess the desire to be very curvy comes from growing up in a neighborhood where curvy women were highly esteemed.

I made the decision to lose the weight I had gained— during my divorce and time of deep depression—the latter part of 2000. I lost it. I wrote this poem in 2001, around the time the weight loss occurred. Subsequently, in 2002 I found out I was pregnant. I gained sixty pounds while pregnant with my youngest son—the most weight I had ever gained in my life. I was such a health fanatic before my pregnancy. However, when I found out I was pregnant I enjoyed myself by eating up everything that was off limits to me before. I declared I would worry about losing the weight after I gave birth. I did just that. After my pregnancy, I lost the weight fast because I breastfed and worked out. However, when I walked away from my jobs in 2005 (salon) and 2006 (NAR), I gained weight again. I was cooking and baking cakes all the time. I really enjoyed being a stay-at-home-mom.

Being unemployed made it difficult to afford gym membership. I walked excessively for exercise and errands because my car had been repossessed. No matter how much I walked, I got bigger and bigger like a blowup doll. I gained twenty-five to thirty pounds. I believe the walking was not rigorous enough for me, and it could have also been the cakes. When I gain weight, I am always in denial before I truly notice the weight gain. I never see or feel the weight coming. I have noticed I gain weight more when I am not very happy about the direction of my life.

I love clothes, but because buying clothes meant I would have to face the fact that I was no longer a size six or eight, I refused to pack my closet with clothes that were not true to me. I have given away some of my smaller clothes, but I have a selected few that occupy my closet today. Now I am working very hard to get back into shape and to stay in shape for life. There was a time I could eat a caramel sundae from McDonald's every day and not gain a pound. Those times are over; my metabolism is like an old rusty cart. It takes a minute to get it going. Hence I have to work hard for a fit body today.

I want to represent God fully, and being in great shape mentally, spiritually, and physically is important for my walk with God. If I am self-conscious about my weight when I go out, it can stifle my confidence; and it has stifled my confidence in certain situations. The lack of confidence can hinder my anointing. I am passionate about my walk with God. Therefore, I have to be passionate about the way I live my entire life. This takes work, but it's work that I am going to do.

If you are healthy and you love who you are, stay the size that you are. Don't allow anyone to make you feel inadequate because of your size. However, if you know that you are not healthy and lack confidence in yourself because of your weight, lose the weight. You only have to satisfy God and you. Remember that <u>life is too great to live like it is too short.</u>

MY BROTHER RAISED ME UP

I have always considered myself powerful
But when someone else recognizes your efforts and
the type of person you are
Their recognition alone can make you feel like a
star
I work hard for everything I have and want in life
I have not gotten to where I want to be
There is still so much I have to accomplish along
my journey
I have found it's not easy
Yet, I keep going and believing
My brother wrote me the other day from his cell
After he read the news I had to tell
He wrote words of inspiration to me
He raised me up and called me a BLACK QUEEN
He acknowledged how hard I work
And how I try to go about things the right way
He acknowledged how people looked up to me and
loved me for the things I would do and say
Reading his words made me feel like I had all the
gold in the world
He had recognized my efforts of trying to break
our family chains since I was a little girl
Do you know how I felt reading the words he
wrote
My knucklehead brother who I fought with time
and time again
Made me feel divine with the words he spoke
I am so happy he sees me for who I am
I am so proud that he has become a man

He loves me for who I am and how I try to
accomplish my dreams
My brother raised me up as a BLACK QUEEN!

I HAD TO LEAVE

I know right now you don't understand
It's obvious what you did wrong
I'm leaving because you went outside of our home
Now you want me to stay and that may be alright
for you
But that's not how it's going to be
Your soul is draining me—causing my soul to
bleed
I am still here if ever you are in need
But now I must say goodbye to you and welcome
in celibacy
I have got to love me more
For the sky I want to soar
I am so tired of dealing with a crazy relationship
I give all of me and through my heart you rip
So understand I had to leave
I have got to be the one who appreciates me for
me!

"It only takes a second to hurt the person you love, but you
can never take that second back."

WORRY-FREE

I don't worry anymore
God carried me through enough in 1999, which
taught me to hold on
I made peace with my father that I loved so much
I have taken out time to know me—with whom I
had lost touch
Any little thing used to bother me
Now I let what will be—be
I don't allow things that I cannot control to affect
me
When I can do something about it, I do
But I don't spend time worrying and making
myself blue
I used to be passive and when someone said
something to hurt me—let it fester inside
Now I stop them in their tracks and take up for
what's mine
I used to want everyone to like me, and that was
crazy
Now I say who cares
Their loss because I'm amazing
I can't worry about people; it's enough that I have
my own fears
So like a woman who has just realized who she
really is
I'm worry-free, and boldly I live!

STRONG BLACK WOMAN AND ALONE

Never did I want to be alone
But it seems to be the best when I come home
After a hard day of work I can rest
No badgering or heavy drama to lie on my chest
I never wanted to be alone, but I can't find that
perfect man
I guess I love too hard and won't settle for less so
they don't understand
I'm not going to give one hundred and fifty
percent and settle for your seventy-five
I don't care what other people say
I want love that is equal to mine
I'm aggressive and strong which some men don't
understand
Perhaps like my father and some men can't
comprehend
I even thought about changing me
But that is ridiculous—this is the way I will be
I can't help that I refuse to take any mess
I don't wait on anyone to do a thing for me when it
comes to my progress
I'm soft and sensitive at the right time
However, I have no patience for games, dates, or
lies
I have dreams and goals that are unusual to most
So my special man needs to be someone who
knows
That he has me, and he doesn't have to worry
Because to him I will always be true
He must be confident and secure

Knows how to love me without me giving him a
clue
He has to be straight with me and play no mind
games
Understand that I work hard because I want fame
Don't feel neglected or draw away because my
work needs me
Instead he loves me as if we've had a drought
whenever he sees me
But until that man finds me
I guess I will just enjoy doing things with my son,
friends, and on my own
I am truly a Strong Black Woman and alone!

"Strong and alone is good, but two soul mates coming
together to create heaven is better."

MY CLIENTS

I love my clients like I love my career
Without my clients what else is there here
My clients are different personalities that make my
days bright
I listen to my clients with secrecy and understand
their plights
My clients can read me like a book if there is
something troubling me
Because my clients know I am normally sweet and
bubbly
I try hard to take care of my clients and their hair
Because my clients are wonderful and beyond
compare
I go out of my way for my clients if I can
But if ever you—my client—feel neglected tell me
I will understand
I value my clients like I value my family
Because my clients are great blessings that God has
brought to me!

I had a few daunting experiences with co-workers in
the hair industry. These experiences really took a toll on
me. When I first got into the hair business I loved it, but
after a while it became a lackluster career. I lost my drive,
and it showed in my work. I completely walked away from
the hair business in 2006 (last salon in 2005) under God's
orders after accepting my call into the ministry. God led
me to Spelman to pursue my college education. God gave
me the fulfillment of an old dream. Matriculating Spelman
was surreal.

Shay Seven

I REAPED WHAT I SOWED
A true apology for something I did in 1995

I am a believer that you reap what you sow at times
So I must surely say **I apologize**
Your man was yours
But he constantly knocked at my door
Checking on me
I was estranged from my relationship
Had pain inside
And along with the pain came the tears I cried
Your man was attracted to me in the beginning
And for a long time I stood my ground
I would close my door and turn him around
Subsequently, he saw a hole
He sat with me while I cried, but things got out of
control
I never slept with your man
I came to my senses before it could go that far
But he still did things to me that led him astray
I apologized for the harm I caused and repented
those sins away
I lay on your man's shoulder, and he kissed my lips
He caressed my body with his soft fingertips
Now I hurt because of what I did to you
I cried tears because that wasn't something I
would normally do
I trespassed on "Private Property"
I crushed your heart while your man comforted
me
I know I was wrong because that man was not
your boyfriend; he was your HUSBAND
And I take responsibility for that

I didn't repent right away, but now I am getting it
back
I will never forget how my heart felt when my
husband broke it in two
But you know what—it made me remember the
hurt I must have caused you
**I'm very sorry because I knew better, and I
disappointed myself
I don't find peace in bringing others death!**

I have always known that married men were off limits
to me—an innate belief. As a woman I felt I had enough
class to get my own man and not leech on to someone else's
husband. However, as a woman I did something that I
wasn't so proud of in 1995. I repented for it. Nevertheless,
I still had to wear the repercussions of my actions (King
David in the Bible is a great example). Sometimes no
matter how much you repent, you have to experience the
repercussions garnered. God will have mercy because of
your repentance.

Marriages should be respected. We must understand
that if we want to be married someday, whatever we have
sowed we will reap. Therefore, if you find pleasure in
cheating with the spouses of others, when you get married
everything you sowed is going to sprout up in your
marriage like a vine and choke you. Whatever you want in
your life, sow it into the lives of others. You may not see it
now, but eventually you will—whether good or bad—it
will show up.

KEDRICK HAS A DREAM

Success for us began when Jesus Christ died
So that means we no longer have to freeload or
step on our brother's or sister's side
To get to where we want to be
God helps us achieve what we want as long as we
have faith and believe
Storms will come, but it's all a test
To make sure that we are worthy and appreciative
of our progress
If it doesn't happen right away, don't worry it
wasn't your season
As long as you gave it your all, you know that you
were not the reason
Try—try again—never give up
Because when it's all said and done God has the
Midas Touch
He can make things appear to happen overnight
So stand firm and never give up the fight
More than anything, God loves a trying man with
dreams
Who stands tall even when everyone vanishes
from his team
If it helps to say I believe in you
Let me express it with my poetry because I do
This is for your desk, so when things seem to get
hard you will remember that God can't fix things
if you give up and let go
He can only raise those up who keep pushing for
the things they believe in and know!

Stay encouraged!

WHY WOMEN CRY

We give all we have, and sometimes we don't
expect anything in return
We get our points across nicely, yet still firm
We love unconditionally and give our families
support
We bear our husbands' children and help hold
down our forts
Some of us take care of our houses, our kids, our
spouses, and work
But now let me tell you why we hurt
We hurt when after all of our years of dedication,
Our spouses and kids show us no appreciation
We hurt when we have given you so many years
of our lives
Have encouraged you through your times of need
and strife
For the kids we taught them all that we could
However, we hurt when they grow up to do no
good
For our husbands we have loved you even when
we didn't understand you
Gave you years of marriages and helped you build
your businesses too
We put our dreams on hold sometimes to give you
support
And after all of that, when you become successful
you want a divorce
Then when one of us becomes depressed and
burns down you and your girlfriend's house
You go to court claiming to be as innocent as a
mouse
Now you know when you look into our eyes

Exactly why women cry!

You will never find a person without baggage. Baggage is simply a negative word for history. However, we must remember not to ignore the signs. All bags do not match! Try putting red old luggage with some new bright orange luggage. We are physically able to see that those bags do not match. This is the same with people and their histories. They don't match enough to come together to form one unit. Some bags may have a little too much history. Some bags may not have enough history. Whatever it may be, we have to recognize the problem and stop forcing what doesn't fit. Some of us see the baggage and know that it is too much for us. Yet, we still allow ourselves to be placed in situations that are not conducive for our health.

SOUL FOOD

Hey my brotha
How are you
Thought I would write this for you
We had our time
You were once my husband
You knocked me off my block my brotha
You made a great mistake
But you realized it was a mistake too late
I hated you my brotha
But God lit up a light so bright in me
And allowed me to be
A strong sista
A forgiving sista
A sista that loves unconditionally
Although I decided to let it go
I want you to know
I wish you the best
Learn from this and give your next love your all
Don't fall
You are my friend and my son's father
So from my heart I forgive you of your turn you
took along our path
What you did does not make you a bad man
I had to realize that we all make mistakes
But we must learn
Please learn!
My brotha, be good to your new sista
Choose a Queen
Treat her like a Queen

Because surely you should know you are a King
Be secure in all you do
Feed your spirit positivity which empowers you
Life is life
And life is living
Love is love
And love is giving
So I give this to you
"SOUL FOOD"

I SAW MY UNCLE'S SOUL DIE

I don't know what it is about this drug-game
How it takes the sweetest people and makes them
act insane
The youngest of ten and I love him so
But his mind is so far out of reach—he has no
place to go
Good-looking—like all my family is—let me tell it
But this drug-game
Which is now his drug-thang
Took my uncle far from this world
I pray because that's all I know to do
But seeing his soul die makes me blue
See, he is physically alive and in his prime
But the drug-game
Which is now his drug-thang
Has my uncle's mind confined!

BLESS IT BE

BLESS IT BE the man that finds me
The man that loves me
The man that cherishes me
BLESS IT BE the man that honors me
The man that respects me
The man that does me right
BLESS IT BE the man that holds me
The man that caresses me
The man that sleeps next to me at night
BLESS IT BE the man that takes care of me
The man that is faithful to me
The man that shares my life
OH BLESS IT BE the man who becomes **my
husband** and makes love to me
The man that kisses these lips
The man that feels the rhythm of these hips
The man that has my every thought
The man that has my love that can't be bought
OH BLESS IT BE,
THE MAN THAT MARRIES ME!

Everyone has baggage. Your parents are baggage. You didn't choose your parents or the things they did before you were born. The way your mother cooked chicken when you were younger is baggage—it sticks with you. Baggage can be huge, small, cute, ugly, good, or bad. The key is we have to learn to live with our baggage in a healthy way or work hard to unload unhealthy baggage. We also have to decide if we can live with the baggage of our significant others before we make huge commitments. **Some bags do not match, and some are too heavy to carry.**

I DON'T DESERVE

I'm a good woman; I work hard and keep a clean
house
So I deserve a man and not a mouse

I don't deserve
A cheesing, game-talking piece of poop
A man who's main objective is not-to-give-a-hoot

I cook big dinners
I can put together a good quick meal
I will tell you what I like and don't like because **I
am REAL**

So I don't deserve
A man who wants to be shady with his money
A man who is only good for you when the days are
sunny

I am a good mother; you will never have to worry
about our babies
And I will respect you and carry myself like a lady

So I don't deserve
A man who can't be faithful and wants to cheat
Or a man who is always running from the police

I am a woman with goals
A woman who respects the head of household

So I don't deserve
A man who doesn't believe in paying the bills
Or a man who hides the way he feels

I am a woman who believes in total satisfaction
A woman who is full of passion

So I don't deserve
A man who will not give me all he's got
Who will not do what it takes to make sure our
marriage stays hot

I deserve
A MAN!
A real man who loves himself and me too
A man who is secure and will not hesitate when he
loves me to say, "I love you"

I deserve
A man and not a boy
I am a woman who deserves the real McCoy

I deserve
A man who gives me a lot of attention
Because I have so many dimensions

I don't deserve
A man who is always telling a lie
A man with concerns to get high

I don't deserve
A man whose entire check is dedicated to child
support
Because then he can't help me hold down my fort

I deserve
A man with mad dividends
So he can hold down his end

I don't deserve
A man who steals
A man who is always eating but buys no food to
make the meals

I don't deserve
A man whose first priority is his car
With a radio in it more valuable than the ride, so
he will never get too far

I don't deserve
A man who has a lot of goals
But doesn't work hard to achieve them so they
turn into mold

I deserve
A man who truly fears God
Loves himself and works hard
Cleaves to his wife and makes his family an
important part of his life
A man who loves unconditionally
Who accomplishes his goals and dreams
And always considers his wife VIP on his team
Who loves his kids
Gives us all the love he has to give
A MAN WHO IS REAL!
Whether it makes me mad, glad, or sad—he will
tell me how he feels
A man who doesn't have a mistress
But constantly gives his marriage his **BEST!**

"You cannot fault a person for loving you the best way they
know how. However, you might have to accept that what
they know is not good enough for you."

...NO LONGER AFRAID TO DIE

Oh how I would cry in my sleep
Dreamt so many times I was falling
For me the fear of death curtailed so many things
It kept me in a box
Where my mind was locked
Hard to penetrate
What will be my fate?
Is this life a waste?
Will I live to see my kids become adults?
God, why would you create me just to die?
Why try?
Where will I go?
When will I go?
How will I go?
God, I don't want to go!
Death had such a hold on me
And I was in church every Sunday
It took a toll on me
The fear never went away
Because I did not trust God
I DID NOT TRUST GOD
After I gave God total control
REALLY GAVE GOD TOTAL CONTROL
Death no longer encapsulated my soul
My apprehension dissipated
I understand
I can comprehend
God's plan
My faith is in God
Much better than the path I used to trod
Death will not be my end
I am no longer a slave to sin

I am the Queen
God called to restore things
Death will only come when I am finished
My life will not be diminished
Jesus freed me long ago
But death—being like Satan—played on me not
knowing the truth
When you don't know the truth it's easy for you to
be duped
I am no longer afraid to die
Because death is not where I will remain
With God is where my soul will reign!

"To know God is to trust him. When you fear death, you
do not know God. When you trust God, you always know
he has something better for you."

I MET AN ANGEL WHEN I LAID EYES ON YOU
Dedicated to D'Wmac

I just can't explain how you would make me feel
It was so unreal
Your glow
Your shine
Something about you that was rather divine
Classic
But suave and cool
Something unbelievable when I laid eyes on you
I saw a shine
I saw a glow
And the way you made me feel—surely
somewhere there was a halo
A pair of wings
Because you made my heart sing
I had no idea what to do
Because I saw God in you
Scared me at first
I was attracted by my thirst
My thirst to feel happy and unique
But still meek
Through you God gave me the energy I needed
and I didn't have a clue
That I had met an angel
When I laid eyes on you

...SURELY YOU KNOW SOMETHING IS MISSING
Dedicated to D'Wmac

If you feel something is missing in your life
I know how you feel
If you feel like sometimes you just don't feel right
The feeling is real
Maybe you think you should be finding you
I know how you feel
If you feel like there is somewhere else you should
be or something else you should be doing
But you don't have a clue
I know how you feel
You feel that way because your spirit knows you
should be here with me
It wants you to come and claim your destiny
It's waiting for you to figure out I am missing
So you can search hard for me and stop disin'
Your destiny
Your spirit longs for me
It's holding on to what you turned away from
Because your arrogance made you appear dumb
Something is surely missing you know
It's me
The promise helps me stay strong and have faith in
our destiny
And with me you are blessed
You will feel peace and solve all your emptiness
Surely you know something is missing

...I LOVE YOU COMPLETELY
Dedicated to D'Wmac

I don't always know why I love you so
I know God put this love I have for you in my
heart
Although you hurt me with the words you said
It's not okay
But I know you don't understand
You are just being an uninformed man
Sometimes God requires us to love completely
without completely understanding
Everything isn't for us to understand
Like our brothers or sisters who do drugs or crazy
things
Or family members who just don't know what
doing "right" means
We still have to love them completely
Without completely understanding
Why they are the way they are
That's what God said, and that's what he means
So just know I love you completely!

Who is D'Wmac? A man I haven't seen in ten years, but a
man I used to pray for every day. I pray for him now when
I think about him.

...LOVE
Dedicated to D'Wmac

I am in love with you
To express how I feel these simple words really
don't do
I wish you were here with me, and I could freeze
the moment in time
Mr. Wmac you blow my mind
I'll take you in my life in an instant
All your idiosyncrasies and peccadilloes can come
too
For you there is no limit to the things I will do
I love your spirit and energy
I love your sensuality
You're the only man who can put me at ease
With you I am comfortable being me
And when I want to get upset you have a spirit that
makes me calm down
You see—I know I will love having you around
You! You! You!
D'Wmac divine
Running acres in my mind
If you could see my heart you would see your face
If I could be holding anyone right now, you would
be all in my space
I love you, and you don't have to put up with
another woman's mess
Because with me you would surely be blessed
"Oh bless it be" the man that marries me and
treats me right

> *And Mr. Wmac you are that man!*

...THE SPIRIT AND SOUL OF A MAN
Dedicated to D'Wmac

You and I
Baby I have your back
I am your other half, and I will never abandon that
Down for whatever when it comes to you
I love and fear God, so you know I will do my best
never to make you blue
I have had unsuccessful relationships
But they too were destine I feel and have gotten me
ready for a lifetime with you
I don't regret my past relationships because I have
learned so much
I have learned to appreciate your touch
The touch of your "Spirit and Soul"
Which is more than an average person can
understand
As a woman, I now realize you haven't really felt
love until you have loved **the "Spirit and Soul" of a**
man.

Love you Mr. Wmac

PUTTING THE PIECES TOGETHER

When you take a look around and go back on all
the things you did
And how all those things dictated the life you live
When you made the decision to further your
education
You recall it was the best move that you had ever
taken
For a while things seemed to get tough
Then suddenly things begin to add up
The weather got much, much, better
Because somehow all the pieces seemed to come
together

"When you do it yourself you cannot be rejected."

BUT GOD

I was born out of wedlock
Had a teenage mother
My father was married to another woman
My mother was eighteen, and my father was
thirty-one
Grew up on welfare
Lived in the projects—Bowen Homes
People getting killed and robbed
Drugs were rampant on the scene
Mother became a drug dealer—to some a B-Town
dope-queen
I remember the sounds of the GBI's breaking down
our door
Officers everywhere
Guns in the air
Guns pointed at me
Until the woman officer screamed
"That's a child!"
Thank God no one was trigger-happy
I wouldn't be here today if they were
God saved my mother from getting prison time
I was elated because I would have lost my mind
If my mother went to prison

We were those Easter kids when it came to church
I had to fight so hard it seemed
Just to have a dream
I was married for the first time at sixteen
First child two months before turning eighteen
Husband got on drugs
Realized I couldn't live off of love
I made so many mistakes

This is not half of my story
Many times I thought it was over for me

But God...
God had a plan for me
The devil tried to make me doubt

But God...
Gave me a way out
You can tell me about everything I have done
wrong

But God...
Changed my song
Yeah, I came from nothing
If coming from something is considered wealth
We were poor

But God...
Has given me the power to get wisdom and wealth
Yes, I have loved two men
I married them
And now I am divorced

But God...
Made me whole
There are no more leaks in my soul
Whenever you talk bad about me
And tell all the things in my history
Don't forget to say...**But God...**

God changed everything for me
In him I am new
I have advantages that I didn't used to

Shay Seven

I am a single mother now
And things are hard
I have cried in the dark
Some days I didn't know how we would make it

But God…
Gives me power
Gives me wisdom for every problem and every
hour
God dries my tears
And whispers his plans in my ears
Therefore I have no fear

I was lost
But God removed the blinders so I could see
God took time to love on me…

You tried to kill me with your talk
I saw your sneers
You can be fake with me
But your spirit reeks how you really feel
I pray for you because I know you have to heal
However, when you talk about me don't forget that
"But God"
God took the **period** you placed behind my life and
made it a **comma**
God made a **"Masterpiece"** out of a life of **drama**
GOD CHANGED ME!
And you are not telling the full story if you don't
tell it right
The **Alpha** and **Omega**
The **Beginning** and **End**
The God of my life that washed away my sins

God took **YOUR period** behind my life and made it
a **comma**
God put the **BUT** behind all the drama
God found use for me
God made this **BLIND** woman **SEE!**

"Seeing is knowing that you need God because God's plan
for your life is essential."

"Life is too great to live like it is too short."

Chapter Two

FICTIONAL AND INSPIRATIONAL SECTION

"God's unconditional love never fails. We just fail to walk in it."

HIV

I don't discriminate
You can be black or white
Living your life right
HIV says here I am
I don't have to know your secrets
I don't care about your dreams
I don't care who doesn't love you
And I don't care who you love
Piercing condoms that fit like a glove
I am not like people; I don't have a specific type
I like red-bones, blackberries, white women,
skinny men, short men, and more
You can be rich or poor
I like pretty legs, small legs, pretty toes, or ugly
toes with a baby toe that leans to the side
You can be an honest person or a person who tells
a lie
You don't have to have long black hair
It can be short or straight
Real or fake
Your sexuality can be heterosexual or gay
You can say you're "bi" if it makes you feel right
Because I don't care how you spend your nights
You can be overweight or have a beautiful
hourglass-shape
I will steal your fate
I sit next to you on the bus
Sit next to you on the train
You can have me and feel no pain
I don't care if you drive an expensive car
I don't care if you are a big movie star
I don't care if you are on the down-low

Shay Seven

Because I am lowdown
You can be a nice little housewife or a woman who
sleeps around
A man with huge muscles in his chest
Or a man who always dresses his best
I welcome them all because I could careless
You can be a child with a beautiful warm smile
Or an old lady
You can have a doctorate degree
That doesn't stop me
You could have been a virgin before you met me
I am that sweet little woman making pies
I am the guy you met on aisle number nine
I'm your Caribbean lover
I am your mother
Your sister
Your brother
I'm the dude you really like
I'm Tom, Bruce, Kyle, and Mike
I am heterosexual, transsexual, gay,
Bisexual, a molester, a dream-killer, and a murder
I'm like Burger King baby—I let you have it your
way
I don't care about your sexuality or how good you
live
I am HIV; you can choose not to acknowledge me,
but I AM REAL!

CANDY CASTLES

Bady was always coming up with some ol' crazy idea. We sat on my porch. Bady sat on this old lawn chair my mother had for years. I sat next to him on a black milk crate. "You know if we could find a million aluminum cans, we would be rich. We could go out every day together and find them." Bady said in a daze. "Bady, shut up! Who wants to spend time collecting a million cans? Not me I tell you. God has other plans for my life. Besides, Mr. Ed only pays a penny a can. So we would have to collect more than a million cans to be rich. Cans stink anyway! Things are going to be sweet for me one day! I just know it is. If there is one thing I have ever known in my life, I know that life is going to be sweet for me." I shot down Bady's plan. "Well, what's your big idea?" Bady asked turning towards me. "I don't know just yet. I know that I will not always be poor. I know that Bady. It's in my heart, right here." I pointed to my chest. "Right here and no one will take it away from me." I gazed out at the trees. "Casin!" My mother called out for me. "Yes Mama." "Time to come in." Mama said. "Okay Mama." "Well, guess I'll see you tomorrow. I have to go myself. Mama told me to be in a little early too." Bady shared. "Okay Bady. I'll see you tomorrow." "Casin!" Mama called again as if I didn't hear her the first time. "Comin' Mama." I ran inside the house. Mama could be so impatient. Oftentimes, I had to have patience for the both of us.

Bady was my best friend. He was a year younger than me. My mother and I lived in the projects in Atlanta, Georgia—for eleven of the twelve years of my life. Bady and his mother must have lived here majority of his life too. We had been best friends since I was in the first grade and Bady was in kindergarten. Bady and I were both the only children of single mothers. At times I considered Bady to be my younger brother because we were just that close. There was never a day I didn't see his face.

It was the beginning of summer. Bady and I didn't really have much to do. We often got with some of the other kids and played kickball or we sat on my porch just talking to each other. Bady and I both had dreams of being rich someday. We saw our mothers struggle. There were times when we desired things that our parents couldn't afford. So we vowed that when we grew up we would be able to afford anything we desired.

I saw Bady from my window as he walked over to my apartment. Knock! Knock! "Mama, that's Bady. May I go outside?" I asked. "Yes Casin, but don't go where I can't see ya." Mama replied. "Okay Mama." I ran halfway out of the door. "Casin, don't let the screen door slam!" Mama yelled in the nick of time. "Okay Mama. Hey Bady." I said walking out of the door. I held the screen door so that it would not rattle Mama's nerves. She hated the sound of that screen door slamming. A lack of home-training is what she thought it represented. "Hey Casin. I got some money." He had a smile on his face. "Do you— how much?" I lifted his hand. "Let's see, about fifty cents for you and fifty cents for me." Bady cheerfully gave me my share. Bady handed me two quarters as our feet automatically turned towards the candy lady's house. He and I shared everything. Whenever we received money, our first stop would be the candy lady's house if the ice cream truck wasn't riding through the neighborhood.

Bady and I walked back to my house licking on our freezes (popsicles in a cup) and holding our other goodies in a bag. "Bady, we don't have any more money." "Of course not. We spent it all like we always do." "Yeah I know. But Bady I was thinking if we plan to be rich someday, we can't keep spending everything we get." "What are you talking about Casin? We are kids—that is what we are supposed to do." He didn't take a break from his freeze. "No Bady, listen to me for a minute. Maybe we can come up with an invention or something if we save all of our money." "Casin, that's crazy." "No Bady. Stop

walking for a minute. Think about it. If we save all the
money we get—we can—we can do something!" "Well
maybe, Casin. I don't know. What are we supposed to do
when we have nothing sweet to eat?" "We can make some
sugar water or our own freezes. If we save all of our
money, one day Bady we can be something!" "Well, I think
it's worth a try—anything is worth a try my mama always
says. I guess I better lick this freeze a little slower. This
might be my last one. No one makes freezes like Ms. Lucy.
I'm going to miss her freezes." "Bady, you are crazy." We
continued walking as we licked our freezes slowly. Ms.
Lucy did make the best freezes. Although I did not tell
Bady, I was going to miss them too.

When Bady and I got back to my house, I went
inside and got one of my mother's old mayonnaise jars.
"Bady, this is what we will put our money in—everything
that we get. We will start with this penny on the ground."
I leaned over and picked up the random penny and placed
it in the jar. "What are we going to do with the money
Casin once the jar is full? Have you thought of that yet?"
"No, but I will come up with something. When I go to
sleep I will dream. Something will come to mind." "Go to
sleep and dream of something to do with our money—is
that normal, Casin?" "I'm normal aren't I? Everyone is
different, Bady." "Yeah but—." I interrupted Bady. "At
least I didn't come up with the aluminum can idea."
"Well, I came up with something. It seemed good to me
while I was thinking it. But I guess it would be really hard
to get rich from saving cans." "Finish your freeze, Bady."
"Let's play checkers once we finish our freezes." "Okay,
I'll go upstairs and get it."

For the entire summer Bady and I saved all the
money we had. We told no one about our money jar. Bady
and I both had birthdays that summer. For our birthdays
we were given a little more money than we would usually
get. We put it straight into our money jar without buying
ourselves anything. Sometimes when he kept the money

jar he couldn't sleep. He thought a burglar was going to break into his house and steal our money jar. It was just like Bady to think such a thing.

At the end of the summer, Bady and I had collected a lot of money. We had to get a bigger jar. This time I got one of my mother's pigs' feet jars. My mother saved all kinds of jars. We would drink out of the small ones. She would store old grease in some of the bigger ones. "Since we have to put it in a new jar let's count it, Bady." "Okay." We counted the dollars first and then the coins. We made four groups of coins: quarters, dimes, nickels and pennies. They were much easier to count that way. "Bady, we have eighty-five dollars!" "Casin, are you sure we counted it right?" "You counted it with me! We have eighty-five dollars! I told you we could do it! I told you!" I was excited. "Casin, you were right! Now what are we going to do with the money? What are we going to do?" "I don't know yet Bady, but we just have to keep saving." "You haven't dreamt yet? It's been all summer Casin, and you haven't dreamt." "No Bady, I haven't dreamt yet. You can't rush God. I'll dream in time." "What does God have to do with you dreaming?" "Once I told my mother a dream, and Bady it came true. So my mother said that God spoke to me in my dreams. Since then Bady that is the way it has been. I will dream. God knows what I want." "I swear you're older than you say you are, Casin." Bady shook his head in disbelief. "Come on, let's get this money in this jar before my mother comes down." I said.

School season rolled around fast. Bady and I were back in school—our summer vacation was over. I had not dreamt of anything. I had no idea what we were going to do with the money we had saved. It didn't worry me that I had not dreamt of anything. I was more worried about keeping Bady patient. He had already been more patient than I ever thought he could be.

Once we started school, Bady didn't ask me anymore whether or not I had dreamt. I guess he figured I would just tell him when I had. One night I finally did dream, and when I awoke I remembered the entire dream. I knew it was the dream that I had been waiting on. In my dream Bady and I were miniature people who lived in houses made of candy. When we went outside of our houses everything around us was made of candy too.

The day after I had the dream was Saturday. I awoke energized. I cleaned up my room and made breakfast for my mother and me. "Mama, I made breakfast." I said as I walked into her room carrying a breakfast tray in my hand. My mother was tired. But she turned over quickly, as if she had been dreaming of food. "Casin, baby this is so nice of you. What do we have here?" She asked as I laid the tray on her legs and climbed in bed beside her. "Right here we have scrambled eggs with cheese like you like it, toast with apple jelly on it, and some fruit. Oh and here—your glass of juice." She kissed me on my nose, and she started to eat. "You are just growing up so." "Mama, I know that sometimes you are tired. But if I had something I wanted to do, would you let me?" "Casin, that depends on what it is." She said in her serious voice. "Well Mama, Bady and I have been saving all of our money since the summer." "What!" "Yes Mama. Last time we counted it we had eighty-five dollars." "Eighty-five dollars!" "Yes Mama. Now Bady and I were thinking of what to do with the money to make it grow. And Mama you know how you said God talks to me in my dreams?" "Yes." "Well Mama, I dreamt that Bady and I were miniature people in a land of candy." "Wow. Okay, so what does that mean?" Mama never stopped eating. "Mama, now don't say anything yet. Wait until you hear everything. I think it means that Bady and I should become a candy lady or a candy man in Bady's case." "What? No, no, Casin." "But Mama, we can do it! You and Bady's mama would only need to help us get the candy. Bady and I can run it when we get out of school." "Casin, a candy-

house?" "Mama, yes! Bady and I can do it, Mama. We
can do it if you let us try." "Well, what about Bady's
mother? What does she think?" "Well, she doesn't know.
Bady and I haven't told her yet. I'm only telling you now
because of my dream. Bady doesn't know I've dreamt. I
will tell him today. I had to tell you first Mama, so that you
could say yes. Please! Bady and I did save the money—that
should show that we are responsible enough." "That is
true, but only if Bady's mother says yes." She pointed at me
with squinted eyes. "Oh thank you Ma," I pounced up and
down "thank you!" "Don't knock over the juice Casin!"
"Oh, I am sorry." I leaped from her bed. "I have got to get
dressed, so I can tell Bady the news!" I said. "Did you
clean your room Ms. Lady?" "Yes Mama. Already ahead
of you. I had to be prepared for your 'yes'. Love you
Mama."

I finished dressing. I was excited to tell Bady about
my dream. "Mama, I'm going over Bady's house." I yelled
as I grabbed a piece of toast and headed out the door. Just
as I was going out of the door—Bady was about to knock.
"Bady! Just the person I was coming to see." "What are
you so happy about?" "Come and sit down in your favorite
chair. Guess what?" "What?" "I dreamt, Bady! I
dreamt!" "What! What did you dream? Tell me!" "I
dreamt that you and I were miniature people, and we lived
in a candy-land." "What? What in the world did that
stupid dream mean? Doesn't sound like a big plan to me."
He laughed. "Bady, the dream is saying that we should sell
candy like Ms. Lucy does! We should become a candy-girl
and a candy-boy!" "Hmmm, that's a great idea. But who's
going to get the candy for us, and whose house will we sell
it in?" "Well, I told my mama everything this morning.
She said if it's okay with your mama—it's okay with her.
We can sell the candy from my house." "I'm sure my
mama won't mind helping with that. Let's go ask her
now!" Bady was excited. He led the way as we ran to his
house.

Bady's mother didn't give us a problem at all about it. In fact, I think she agreed faster than my mother. Bady's mother couldn't believe we had enough self-control to save money. After we talked with Bady's mother, our mothers called each other. They agreed to alternate whenever it was time to take us to the store to replenish our supplies. Later that day my mother took us to the store to buy our candy, cookies, sodas, and ice cream pops. When we got home Bady and I sat down and made a pricelist. "Okay Bady, now this is the hardest part to me. We have got to come up with the prices for the goodies we will sell." "Um—well I think you better do that part, and I will write it down." "Okay, write it neat Bady. Well, Ms. Lucy is right around the corner and the ice cream man still comes in the neighborhood every day. So we have to do something Ms. Lucy and the ice cream man don't do. We can make our prices ten cents lower than their prices. That way we will still make a thirty percent profit and gain more people to buy from us because our prices are lower. Yeah, that's it!" "Good idea, Casin! You are a regular businesswoman." We giggled. Bady and I got our pricelist together. We arranged our candy on my mother's kitchen table. Everything looked really nice once we finished. We were officially running our own business!

"Whelp Bady, we did it. Isn't the table beautiful?" "Now we need to make an open and closed sign like Ms. Lucy has." "Great thinking Bady! I have a red marker and some construction paper upstairs. I'll go get it." Bady made the open and closed sign. He was very good with things such as that. He stuck a hole in the top of the sign with scissors and cut some string from one of my old toys. He hung the sign on a nail that was already protruding out of my mother's door. You could see the sign several feet away from the house.

When we went to school that Monday, Bady and I told all the kids about our candy-house. Before we could get home and put our books down, kids who wanted to buy candy surrounded the house. Although we were running our own little business, our mother's made sure we established a set opening and closing time. They wanted to make sure we would have time to do our homework and chores. The first month of being in business Bady and me profited one hundred and fifty dollars. Our mothers were very shocked. They didn't hesitate to take us to the store to restock our candy. Bady and I told our parents that we wanted to save our money. They agreed and got us a savings account together that we couldn't touch until we were both eighteen years old.

Selling candy was more than an adventure. It was fun too, and we took it seriously. We were able to make our own money, run a business, and test all the new candy that came out. However, we were careful not to eat much of our products. Bady and I sold candy for five years—until I graduated high school. Bady graduated a year later. We both went to cosmetology school after high school. The year Bady graduated cosmetology school we removed our savings from our account and invested in owning a salon. Bady and I had saved over $7000 just from selling candy as children. Whenever our clients ask us how we got the name for our salons, we tell them this story. Many laugh because it is unbelievable to them. Yet, it is a reality for Bady and me. Selling candy was the start of what allowed us to move our mothers out of the projects. Today Bady and I at the age of twenty-four and twenty-five own four salons in different locations around Atlanta. We named them all "Candy Castle I-IV."

THE END

"Anything is possible if you achieve to believe."

WOMAN

I know dog gon' well you are not trying to play me
dumb
Do you know the power I possess
Do you know the power of my charm
I don't think you realize why God made me
He made me to help you see
I am the "world" sweetie
So stop being so high on yourself
Stop acting as if about me you don't care
I can bear your children
You can't bear mine
Yes, you have what it takes to help make a child
But God gave me the hard job of carrying it
Because I was more competent
Yeah, yeah, you bring home the bacon
But I fry it like no other
If you don't act right, you can take your bacon
along with your bags home to your mother
You better recognize me for who I am
Recognize that without me you don't know what it
is to fully be a man
I'm tired of you abasing me
You're gonna miss me if I leave
I suggest you love me like God had planned
And recognize that you are nothing without
WOMAN!

SHE FOUND LOVE ON THE GRAVEYARD SHIFT

Lonely but beautiful and so much to gain
She had one problem, and Ricky was his name
He was jealous of her and her big brown legs
He did bad things to her that made her scared
She was smart; her mother thought she'd be
something someday
But her mother had no idea that Ricky would steal
her fate
She moved in with Ricky because he wanted so
much more
Ricky promised to marry her, and their love would
soar
One day her mother visited their apartment
During her mother's entire visit, in her bed the girl
spent
She told her mother she was not feeling so well
She covered her bruises, so her mother could not
tell
How Ricky had beaten her the night before
She was young and would cover up anything for
the man she adored
When her mother left the house Ricky's neighbor
called to her and said,
"Excuse me, but are you that girl's mother?"
"Yes, I am." Her mother replied.
"Do you know your daughter screams every
night?
I have seen other girls come and go because of
how he beats them so.

Get your daughter out of there before he takes her
away from here!"
Her mother turned around and knocked back at
Ricky's door to talk to her daughter after what the
old lady said
The talk did no good, and four days later the dear
lady's daughter was dead
Her love for Ricky was like driving off a cliff
Because **SHE FOUND LOVE ON THE GRAVEYARD
SHIFT!**

MY BEST FRIEND

I have known you all of my life
You are my best friend
I would give you anything
You are the only woman I allowed in
You tell me all your secrets, and I tell you all of
mine
We are like blood sisters, and that is hard to find
I watched your kids; they call me auntie
I am like their second mother; they love me
I got married, and you were right by my side
You wished me happiness, and together we cried
I thought to myself
My life is going well, and I am so fulfilled
Until one afternoon I had some time to kill
I thought I would surprise my husband with some
Chinese food for lunch
But instead I walked up on him having my best
friend for brunch
I fell to the floor with tears in my eyes
My world tumbled down full of lies
I can remember seeing him on top of you
The two most important people in my life
Whoever would have knew
My heart crushed into pieces
How could you two do me like that
I almost lost my mind, and God had to help me
capture it back
You took away all of our good memories with one
catastrophe
The two of you lost the best person in your lives
when you lost me.

RIVER FLOW

I cry tears of pain
I cover my eyes because they show shame
I feel hurt, lonely, and lost
I cry tears of pain—I cry tears
I have been hunted, trapped, and violated
Wrongly done and intimidated
What I fear I'll tell no one—keep my tears inside
Oh, how hard I cry
Can you see through my shell
Can you tell I've been through hell
Do you want to comfort me and help me find
peace of mind
Well, loving people like you are the reason I cry
these tears I cry.

Sandra was a hardworking college student who decided to take a break from her studies to attend a friend's party. At the party her best friend's boyfriend and two of his fraternity brothers raped her. Out of her hurt and pain, she decided not to report the rape. She tried hard to act as if it never happened. As time passed, Sandra's English professor could see that she was having some problems. Sandra could feel his detection. The more the professor wanted to help, the more Sandra pulled away. Sandra was afraid to trust anyone after the rape. She eventually dropped out of college and got hooked on drugs.

BUTTERFLY

Oh how I long to be free
Flying places I never thought I would see
Leaving a part of me every place I go
Yet taking knowledge from the places I have flown
When I'm tired and ready to rest
With the angels shall be my quest
Wise and old from the long journey my wings
have flown
With the angels I shall go home
Peace, love, and harmony
With my God, I shall finally be free!

A KISS

Someone once said a kiss was just a kiss.
I don't find that to be true.
A kiss is like a thirsty flower wet from dew.
A kiss is the start of so many things.
A kiss can be the start of a woman getting an
engagement ring.
A kiss can comfort a child when they need it most.
A kiss can connect people from coast to coast.
A kiss can be full of heart.
A kiss can bring light to someone's dark.
A kiss can be mild or full of emotion.
A kiss is the start of all love potions.
I just cannot agree that a kiss is just a kiss.
A kiss can bring the world so much bliss!

FULL-FIGURED, BEAUTIFUL, AND HAPPY

I don't wait around at parties for someone to ask
me to dance
I don't stuff myself in small pants
Thing is, I am full-figured and beautiful
There is nothing about me that I don't love
I don't need a man in my life to make me feel
blessed
Truth is, I don't need his criticism or his mess
If he can't love me for me
Then with him is not where I want to be
See, when God made me he knew exactly what he
had in mind
There's more of me so with his perfection he spent
more time
Therefore, I will not let society make me feel like
on this earth I shouldn't be
I am **FULL-FIGURED, BEAUTIFUL, AND HAPPY.**

MAN, OH MAN

I sit and I think about how blessed the world was
when God created man
Strong cheekbones and powerful hands
A chiseled body and a brain to think
Deepness in his voice when he speaks
A rib from his body to create his mate
Soft and sensual woman, whom he appreciates
The tears that fall from his eyes when he's in pain
The smile that spreads across his face when he
experiences gain
There is nothing like a man
For he is truly a blessing for a woman to
understand.

...A REMARKABLE WOMAN

I am who I am
That's really all I can say
When men look at me, their eyes become dazed
I don't know what it is about me
I have this glow
Which attracts men from coast to coast
To be honest, I really feel it's my spirit
God shines from inside of me
Which have men trembling
I am who I am
And that's all I stay true to
Being true to myself makes me irresistible to you,
you, and you
I'm sure it's not the swivel in my hips
Or my voluptuous lips
It's the inside of me
My spirit
My personality
God's shine
My mind
Beauty is not simply skin-deep with me
It's more of my heart
My soul
Not my clothes
Or my shoes
It's how I carry myself and the things I do
I am beautiful because of the spiritual being I am
I stand before you a "Remarkable Woman!"

THE BOY WITH A GUN

He grew up in the ghetto
He was doomed from the beginning they say
He had several chances but chose the wrong way
He had to be hip and hang with the guys
He eventually experienced so much that he had
hate in his eyes
He didn't have his father, and he was too
disobedient for his mother
He knew the dope dealers and street thugs as his
brothers
Life got very hard, so he decided to buy himself a
gun
He killed a man and from there he was on the run
He had nowhere to go—nowhere to stay
He hid in the alley—crying like a baby
He was living on the streets, and the cold was
cutting him like a knife
He put the gun to his head and at sixteen years-old
took his life.

MY LONELY HEART

Some may say that love is not everything
But I think it is
I know the joys love brings and how it makes you
feel
The uniting of souls
Love and togetherness
Companionship and sharing of goals
My lonely heart has yet to be shared
Where could love be?
Is it that love doesn't love me?

Teresa is a model in her late thirties. She has traveled
all over the world and met many people. She's affluent and
famous. However, she has no one to share her life with.
She often smiles as if she is the happiest person in the
world. Yet, inside she is a lonely little girl. She is beautiful,
and she's had many relationships. However, she is often
attracted to the wrong men. Teresa has been used and
abused by the men in her life. True love evades her. This
produced a void in her life. For consolation, she spoils
herself with fancy things and surrounds herself with family
and good friends. Although she appears to have so much,
she lacks the very thing she wants the most.

A FIST

You didn't think I saw you crying, but I did.
I heard your screams last night and your kids.
Why do you let him hurt you this way?
Do you think he'll just stop beating you someday?
Well, he won't if you don't leave him alone.
You are a queen, and he's beating you off of your throne!
You don't need him; he's no good for you!
There is nothing he does for you that you can't do.
Don't keep him around for the sake of having a man!
He showed you he doesn't care; and he'll never understand
He doesn't have to beat you to get things accomplished.
Communication is the key, and it doesn't start with a fist!

Shadrea was a young schoolteacher who got involved with the wrong man. He beat her every night, but for love she thought it was something she could stand. Her co-worker was her neighbor. She heard Shadrea and her kids scream every night. She advised Shadrea to get rid of her boyfriend. It took a few bumps and bruises. However, Shadrea came to her senses and got rid of that no-good man!

WHERE IS LOVE

There are so many wonderful things you do
The person that you are and the person you have
become
Just what you mean to me may truly be a fantasy
I am caught up in the moment
Yet lost in the passion
I suffer from guilt for holding you so near
When my feelings are so far
Years of hard work and dedication
But no matter how hard I try
Love for you I cannot find

Stacy and Antonio were married for twenty years.
They were married when Stacy was eighteen, and Antonio
was thirty-eight years-old. Antonio married Stacy after her
parents died in a car crash. He promised that if she would
be his wife he would always take care of her. Well,
Antonio did just as he promised. Stacy was grateful to him.
However, no matter how hard she tried, she never loved
Antonio the way she thought a wife should love her
husband.

FUNNY FACE

My eyes are large and dark, not light like others
My skin-tone probably the darkest you've ever
seen
Pug-nosed, not pointed nor perfect
My lips are thick, but I've learned men look at
them as voluptuous
My teeth are not so straight, but my smile helps
them out
I've learned to accept me where you probably have
not
I've searched hard for my soul, although people
have tried so hard to bury it
I've learned that I can do whatever I want to do in
life
There is nothing in the air to stop my flight!

Rachel is a young African-American woman. When she was a girl, she always felt bad about herself. Society treated her differently from white girls and the lighter-skinned black girls. As she grew older she gained self-esteem, knowledge, and determination. She gained beauty that shined from the inside-out. With her so-called imperfect looks she rose to the top. She became a very successful Neurosurgeon who made a difference in the world for all races of people.

Shay Seven

WINE-O

I thought of the color of green
For wanting it was never what it seemed
Perhaps it would make my box bigger
My smile probably wider and my old rusty cart
shine
I could have my own bottle of booze
And for my newfound friends expensive wine
I would get rid of this old coat and buy new shoes
But still the color of green could not kill my blues

John is from a small suburban town in California.
From one bad investment he lost everything. Subsequently,
his high society friends turned their noses up at him. He
had to live on the streets. He started drinking
uncontrollably. Consequently, he became known as the
town-drunk. None of his rich friends vowed to help him.
In fact, many of them pretended as if they didn't know him
when they saw him. John was hurt, and he realized that
his wealth created a life for him that was a façade. When
the money dissipated the façade disintegrated. John had to
face his greatest fear—money made the man.

MY DROWNING HEART

Can I awake by myself again!
Does it always have to be two?
Will my life always be this way?
Is this my punishment for loving you?
Can I cry alone?
Do you always have to know my hurt and my
fears?
I know I should be happy to know that your love is
here!
A commitment I've made for a lifetime—have I
really!
This is too much for me!
Okay, could I be crazy?
I have something that is truly amazing.

Blake had only been married a year. His wife was his dream-wife, but at times Blake felt as if he had signed his life away. He had spent so many years alone. It was very difficult for him to get used to being married. However, he had moments where he realized he was just being selfish. He knew he had a wonderful wife. Concerned about his inability to adapt to marriage, Blake went to his pastor for counseling without telling his wife. From that point on, he worked very hard every day to be a great husband.

IT'S SO HARD TO FIND A GOOD MAN

Lord, it's so hard to find a good man
Just when you find one and you think he is good
He never does the things he said he would
Men talk about women being fake
But after you commit to one, he makes you feel like
you made a mistake
Men are never who you thought they were
They become evil and vindictive
Have wives and mistresses
Have eight kids when they said they had none
Claimed they had two jobs, and they don't even
have one
They bragged about their houses, and claimed
they're huge
When they actually live in apartments with no
food
Claimed the fancy cars they drive are theirs
Later on you find out they belong to the neighbors
upstairs
They floss with big bankrolls when they take you
out
But they haven't paid their bills yet, so they have
no clout
Want you to laugh at their lame jokes
Then get mad when you tell them you are ready to
go
They try to tell you what you need to do with
yourself
As if they are perfect and need no help
Make suggestions how you should wear your hair
When they give up no money, so why should they
care

Cheat on you with every woman they can
But when you get smart they claim they'll be good
men
Lie to you when they know you will find out
But they continue to lie no matter what it's about
Won't ever tell you they love you first
Want you to feel their love is the only one to
quench your thirst
Want to take you out and sit you in the back or
take you out-of-town
So you know something no-good is going down
All some of us women want is an honest, devoted,
loving-hand
But it's just so hard to find a good man!

IT'S NOT HARD TO FIND A GOOD MAN

I hear women say they can't find a good man
Well, here I am
But you pass over a good brotha like me
Seems you like the so-called thugs with the gold
teeth
I am not with the gold teeth, but I can treat you
right
I am a real man
With a real plan
I have goals, and I am not a big talker
I will show you attention, but I am no stalker
I will call you and make you smile in the middle of
the day
I will send you flowers and have sweet things to
say
I will not be selfish and want you to do everything
for me
I will treat you the way God intended things to be
And I will demand you be treated the same by
everyone else
Because hurting you would be like hurting myself
I will take care of your kids if they come with the
package
Do whatever—just leave all the baggage
I will love you right; you will never be able to
compare me to another
I will make you feel like a woman—become your
number-one lover
I will pay attention to your body—of course then
you will be my wife
Because I have God as head of my life
See, I was made just for you

When God's creations come together we are one
and no longer two
So tell me why you are looking so hard for a good
man
Like I told you in the beginning—here I am!

"Sometimes we are so focused on getting what we want out
of our lives that we fail to see the value of the people in our
lives."

…I IS WHAT I IS

I feel comfortable being me
My mistakes and all make me complete
I can't put up a front for you
I is what I is
And I don't apologize for that
I is what I is
And that I will not retract
God makes no mistakes
Therefore I love me
I is what I is
And that is all I claim to be!

...YOU HAVE TO HAVE THE ROOT

Life is hard
But if you believe in God
It will soon go your way
You have to have faith
Things will happen
Sometimes you will get down
You will have the desire to vacillate
And from my experience—sometimes you may
However, you can correct things if you repent and
pray
You will get back on track and water the root
The root that is always there
Implanted inside of you
You cannot pull up the root

The root of faith!

The root that tells you if your desires are of God
You will have what you say
The root tells you God is there
Waiting on you to open up and overcome your
fears
The root allows you to know that although things
don't happen today
God is churning things for you to see a better way

God is the root!

And God is inside of us all
Nourish God in us and we will never fall
God is the root
Although we may not always see sunshine

We must not pluck out the root, and good things
will come in time
It takes the **sun** and the **rain** to produce
"good fruit"
<u>**Remember always that God is the root!**</u>

GIVE IT TO GOD

Sometimes things just don't go right
Sometimes you don't know w why
You may feel sad and hurt inside
It helps to cry
But the best thing that ever helped me
And I will tell you because I know you're going to
be
Alright
Give it to God
Don't let your problems weigh you down
Don't find joy in moping around
Give it to God
If it's a load
And I know it is
Come talk to me, but first talk to God
God can give you what I can't
There might be some things going on in your life
that I cannot comprehend
I won't judge you because I am your friend
But the best thing to do is to give it to God
God will know what to do
And God will see you through
Might seem a little redundant
But…
Give it to God

...GOD, ONE MORE DAY

God, give me another day
Another day to repent and to pray
Another day to fulfill my dreams
Another day to believe
Another day to love
And have love love me
Another day to help someone less fortunate
Another day I will never regret
Another day to love my family
Another day for me to be me
God, please give me one more day!

EMBRACE YOUR DREAM

When you look to the stars
You look deep to see
All the things that help you have faith and believe
All the things that make you fight harder
When you're out of breath but have more stairs to
climb
You think of all the things that make you feel
blessed and refined
So that you can climb another stair once you've
caught some air
You acquire more strength because you know
what will take you there
But when it gets harder and you want to scream
With your heart and soul **"EMBRACE YOUR
DREAM!"**

"Dream-killers are faithful, so you have to be faithful to
bring your dream to life. Dream-killers come in all forms
and facets. They are in the church, at school, at work, at
home, and in your inner circle. Dream-killers are always
people you know because people you don't know cannot
kill your dream. Dream-killers are always those 'buzzards'
you have on your team. They are disguised as Eagles. True
Eagles don't get mad because you fly. Eagles like having
other Eagles by their side."

SUDDENLY

Suddenly I can see so much
My eyes are opened wide
Things I didn't understand
I now understand
I can relate
My mind is open
I have empathy
Suddenly I know what you mean
Because it has happened to me
Suddenly
Things have come together for me
I know what I want to be
Suddenly
I know what love is
I know whom I love
And it was overdue
Suddenly
I know more about me
Which allows me to better understand you
Suddenly
I know it's not all about me
But it's up to me
It's God's plan
It's my future
Suddenly
I know I'll have troubles
I know I'll have trials
And if I need it—I will have my time to mope and
cry
But then suddenly
I'll rise
Like the warrior I am

With strength, wisdom, and courage
Strength to rise and try again
Wisdom to know how to navigate
Wisdom to pray my fate
Courage to withstand any obstacle in my path in
order to accomplish my dreams
Courage to be free
Courage to be me
Suddenly…I see…

"You can understand a lot after you have gone through
something."

A MAN CRIES

I know I am a man
But sometimes I have pain
And I don't handle mine the same
But there are times I feel I am going to lose my
mind
I have problems too, and sometimes I understand
things you don't
I will do things you think I won't
I am just a man
But if you try me, I'll show you I understand
Sometimes I cry
And that's real
Crying is a reflection of how I feel
You may not physically see my tears
I am good at crying inwardly
When I explode, I imploded first
So don't think you're in it alone
Sometimes I cry when things hurt or go wrong
I vowed to make you happy
So when the bills are not paid and we don't
accomplish the goals we made
You don't have to nag me to make me understand
I can comprehend
And it's harder for me because I feel I don't have
anyone to talk to
I don't want to burden you
A man was told he should be able to handle things
on his own
Now I know that is wrong
So when I tell you I understand or know how you
feel
Don't think I am placating you and not being real

Sometimes I cry
I make mistakes
I realize the way I handle things are not so great
But allow me to grow
Allow me time to think
You don't have to hassle me
When my mother and wife don't agree
And you split me like a twig to make me see
Your point
DON'T ASK ME IF IT BOTHERS ME
IT DOES
It bothers me when the woman that birth me and
the woman that shares my babies cannot get along
I want a happy home
I know when the bills are due
I know if I don't give you the money the creditors
will sue
So when I am out of work
Know that I hurt
I am not a machine
I am a man
You may think because I don't break down I don't
understand
But I do
I handle mine a little different than you
This man sighs
This man also cries…

…INVINCIBLE

I can't explain where my strength comes from
I know it must be God
It must be the love he has for me
Because whenever I fall I get up
Whenever I cry I wipe my tears and find reasons
to smile
When I am confused, it doesn't last long
I stay true to me because when I sing a sad song
I am the only one there who really knows the hurt
Of course God knows
But physical beings don't know
They can't really understand although they say
they can
I don't expect them to
I say with age this thing called life gets easier
It does for me
Because I know it's a learning experience and
every day that I live
As I learn–it gives
Gives me what I need
And along my journey
I discovered that I am **INVINCIBLE!**

IF LOVE WERE

If love were a beautiful blue sea,
I would be deep in it
Resisting the rescue crew trying to save me
If love were the corner of my room,
I would be the line where the ends of the walls
meet
If love were my grandma's rocking-chair,
I would rock in it—constantly falling asleep
If love were a school,
No matter the subjects or studies—that is where I
would be
I'd be in every class, and nothing would distract
me
If love were sugar, surely I would be the cane
If love were a dreary cloud, surely I would be the
rain
Wherever love be
I would be the next thing.

THE ONLY WAY I CAN LOVE YOU

I love God
That is the only way I can love you
You claim you love God, but you hate me
You do everything in your power that you think
would cause me pain and misery
Yet, you love God
How can you love someone you have never seen
But you can't love me
I didn't say it
God did
You claim you read God's word
I don't think you interpret it right
Perhaps you choose not to obey it
You have done a lot to me
But I don't wish any bad to you
In fact, I pray that God's word penetrates your
heart
And slice away
All that is dark
If I love him
Although it might be hard, I must forgive and love
you
I don't get my kicks out of taking revenge and
hiding my hands
Because of the evil things you do!

"Trust God to be your vindicator."

I WISH I COULD FLY

I don't know what I feel
And sometimes I don't know why
When I become this way I wish I could fly
I drift away from the day
Sometimes I just meditate
Meditate so long I fall asleep
Meditation helps me find peace
Sometimes I hurt endlessly
I cry so much inside
When I cry I wish I could fly
I want so much to be happy
Accomplish my goals
Uplift my spirit and soul
I feel helplessly inclined
Sometimes I feel God and I don't see eye to eye
So I close my eyes and I begin to fly
I fly where everything is where I want it to be
Only positive and beautiful things surround me
People love each other
Good people that died are with us again
There is beautiful light and no end
God is there, and we surround his glow
His son Jesus is there purifying all souls
When my time is up
I open my eyes
Squeezing them back, so that I can continue to fly!

DON'T CHANGE A THING FOR ME

If you look in the mirror and you're happy with
what you see
Then don't change a thing for me
Be happy with who you are
It doesn't matter what I say, as long as you think
you are a star
If I say I don't like the way you dress
It doesn't matter as long as you feel like a success
Don't change a thing for me
If your hair isn't pleasing to me
But your hair makes you happy
Then don't you change a thing for me
Be you and let it be
Don't you dare change a thing for me
And don't let me rain on your parade
Not one day
Hold your head up high
High enough to touch the sky
And~don't~you~dare~change a thing for me!

MORE THAN A SURVIVOR

LIFE

Let's talk about life
Life can throw a horseshoe in just when
everything seems so perfect, so planned
Life can sometimes get to the point it seems it's
working more against you than for you
Suppressed, stressed, or depressed
Whatever, still it's a building to climb
Sometimes a catastrophe that makes you lose your
mind
However, I demand "Life" gives me the best it has
to offer
God said his kids shall possess the land
And I am his child so "Life" realizes I am more
than just a "Human"
I am why the word "Life" exists
Therefore, why should I settle for anything less
than bliss
I would be remiss
I am "Life"
So "Life" will never be misery to me
I shall have "Life" and that more abundantly!

...I PRAY

When you seem so confused
What do you do?
I pray
And I pray
Sometimes my answers don't come right a way
In fact, I think they elude me
Although, I've heard some say they're right on
time
Hearing that doesn't ease my mind
I hate not knowing what to do
I hate when I feel nothing belongs
I abhor being blind
It's not important to me what anyone else feels
But I have got to be happy
I have got to feel whole
Until then there is nothing that will rest my soul
I have got to look around and see things that make
me feel glee
All this poison is disrupting the being I am
The person I know I should be
I have to find PEACE
I don't want to die to have it
I just don't
I want to enjoy my life right now
Right here
On Earth
So I pray...

DOORMAT

I cooked you meals perfectly seasoned
I ironed your clothes
So what could be the reason
I plucked hairs out of your chin when they were
ingrown
I made sure you returned to a clean home
So what could be the reason
I advised you when you needed it
When you didn't want to be bothered
I didn't force what didn't fit
I was there for you throughout all
Whenever you needed me all you had to do was
call
I was there!
No hesitation
I was there!
No "wait a minute Baby"
I was there!
If I had to drive a country mile
I was there!
Now you act like you don't remember
Didn't give me a birthday gift, and it's December
My birthday was August
I needed a ride when my car was broken and you
told me to catch the bus
As if you work too hard to give me a ride
Dude, you work part-time
All of a sudden you just flipped on me
Are you trying to tell me something
Have I gained weight, and you think I'm too fat

Or is it because you were using me as a doormat?

THESE WALLS

I can't breath
There is something wrong with me
These walls are torture
I have got to get out of here
I am tired
I am blue
My mind isn't thinking about a thing
Life is disappointing me
My soul bleeds
These walls!
They are closing in on me
I got to get out
Where I can be
Free!
These walls are full of negativity
I can't see!
I can't see clearly
My brain is cluttered
Oh God help me
I can hear my heartbeat
Faster and faster!
These walls are a disaster!

...DELICATE FLOWER

She is strong
Oh, yes she is
Working day by day
And taking care of her kids
She is everything to everyone
Loving
Considerate
Encouraging
Fun
Quite a lady
Yet full of power
But deep inside she is surely a delicate flower!

Shay Seven

MY HEART

I have to look above sorrow
Tell all misery to flee
My heart is vulnerable
Fun-loving and meek
It loves so easily
But when hurt, it crumbles into pieces
Pieces that are abrasive
Abrasive because of hate
No, no, I didn't mean hate—hurt
Or did I really mean hate?
After "hurt" surely comes "hate"
But my heart soon realizes "hate" is not of my
Creator
So it releases "hate" and comes back to love
MY HEART
Just never gives up…

NEW WORLD SHEROES

I stand before you fighting for every cause I feel
should be fought for
I don't make my color an issue
Because I am a woman who's on a mission
I have a chance now; therefore, I am going to
make more than the best of it
Don't get upset when you tell me something, and I
go behind you and check it
I have to confirm things on my own
I'm making history, and several women come with
me
I am not alone
We must make sure we are working with facts
We have a job to do, and mere fiction can hold us
back
We have to pave a way for our gender and our
kids
We are changing history with every day that we
live
We live!
PROPHETESSES
POETS
DOCTORS
LAWYERS
PREACHERS
TEACHERS
ATHELETES
THESPIANS
AUTHORS
COSMETOLOGISTS
MUSICIANS
GRAPHIC ARTISTS

MOTHERS
WIVES
DAUGHTERS
We have brains
We have plans
Putting businesses up wherever there is land
Nothing can stop us now
We are the future
And the future is US
We are saving our own day
We are our own heroes
Because we are **POWERFUL WOMEN OF GOD, we**
are certainly "THE NEW WORLD SHEROES!"

GOD GIVES ME THE STRENGTH TO MAKE IT
THROUGH

Life is so hard but I…
Got to make it through

I get tired of my job but I…
Got to make it through

I don't have a love in my life
But I'll be alright
Because I…
Got to make it through

My feet hurt, but I still have one more day of work
and I…
Got to make it through

I feel so alone
I stare at the walls in my home

A DIVERSIFIED BLACK WOMAN: I FEEL SO BLESSED

Looking and trying to come up with some answers

No answers appear
But still I live so I...
Got to make it through

And I will
With every day that I live
God gives me the strength to make it through!

A WOMAN'S CHILD

Nothing can compare to a mother's love
No matter how her child is, to a mother he or she
is as beautiful as a dove
A woman's child
Cross-eyed or perhaps crooks in his or her teeth
Pigeon-toed and when he or she walks his or her
feet meet
Maybe not as attractive and perhaps an imperfect
smile
But I tell you what that's still that woman's child
Carless
Worst dress
A straight financial mess
But still that is that woman's child
If she talks about 'em, just listen and smile
Irrespective of what he or she has done
That's still that woman's child!

"A mother's love should never be conditional but
unconditional like God's love for us."

ALMOST DOESN'T COUNT

I saw the sun and the moon in your eyes
The very first day that you walked by
You seemed to be so special to me
God-fearing
You were so fly
We grew special to each other
I told you I loved you
You "almost" told me you loved me too
But it didn't come all the way out
Did anyone ever teach you that "almost" doesn't
count
I gave you my heart
I could tell you almost gave me your heart too
But other girls were around
For your "almost" they were going to stay down
Baby, "almost" doesn't count in God's world
I am a God-fearing woman and not an asinine girl
I need more than what "almost" can bring
You "almost" said you would marry me
You were at the jewelry store "almost" about to
pick out the engagement ring
But who was going to hold on for that
"Almost" doesn't consist of any facts
I "almost" believed you
I "almost" stayed
However, you see I'm not there
Because "almost" leads to another way
I need an "I do" kind of guy
So my almost-was-going-to-stay-with-you led into
a factual goodbye!

…ONE LAST CRY

I missed you last holiday
It just doesn't seem to be real
You're not here with me
I love you, and you just turned away
I know things were imperfect, but I loved having
you here with me
I had you here when I needed someone to talk to
When my days at work didn't go right, it made me
feel good to come home to you
Now I feel so alone
And I still don't believe you're gone
Without you I just don't seem to be living
I am breathing
Breathing it seems without a reason
Although we have said our goodbyes
I guess I have to have this one last cry.

MADE-UP

Who are you?
Made-up into a hopeless clue
With your fancy clothes
And your new nose
Your beautiful $200 shoes
And your weave-do
Who are you I ask you still?

With your big bank account
And all your clout
With your artificial looking wife
Who stays under a doctor's knife
Your fast sports car
Driving around looking like an overpaid star
Who are you?
Do you have a clue?

Or are you too busy being made-up?
Made-up of society's mess
Trying to add up but causing you stress
Instead of being happy being you
You remain made-up into a hopeless clue!

LOVE ME AND HELP ME

I get so tired of you calling me fat
Criticizing me like you are all of that
Every time you lift me up, you let me down
I am so tired of you being around
You met me when I was small
You said for better or for worst
Now I guess someone else is quenching your thirst
Because you are never here
And when you're here you have me in tears
Walk with me if you want me to lose weight
And how about changing your eating habits
instead of every night requesting steak
When I am cooking you steak, I want steak too
So it's hard for me if you won't do
Things with me
We are married, and it shouldn't be
Hard for you to see
That maybe if you step in
Take my hand
I wouldn't feel so bad
I love me
I never stopped
I guess you did
But if you think you are not in love with me
anymore
You need to leave me in peace and make use of the
door!

A MAN AND HIS MOTHER

I can't deal with you and your crazy ways
See, you don't respect your mother, and to me that
is important
A man who loves his mother, will love me
A man who has been nourished, will nourish our
family
I don't care if she made you mad
That's your mother, and to me your disrespecting
her is sad
Mothers should be loved
They are heaven sent
If you respect your mother, that gives me a better
chance
Of you respecting me and being a great man
A man who disrespects his mother will certainly
have no respect for me
I am sorry, but that's what I believe
If you call your mother a bad name
I know you will call me one
If you have no love in your heart for her
I know our love is done
If his mother is in his life
I watch how he treats her
Because it's signifies how he will treat his wife.

I'M GONNA DO YOUR TIME WITH YOU

Baby, I miss you
But see I don't want you to worry about me
I am going to be strong
I won't start a new
Because I 'm gonna do your time with you
So what you will be gone three years
You and I have loved each other longer than that
I didn't come this far just to turn back
I know you miss me
I miss you too
Just think of all the things we used to do
It does a lot for me
I mean, I know sometimes it's not good
reminiscing
But it warms my heart
Although I end up crying in the dark
I don't care because I am going to be okay
It's been 565 days
We don't have much longer now
Ray-Ray don' grew up
And Bo-Bo got his lowrider truck
Tricia is pregnant by Rick
And the rap game don' happened to Nick
Your mama is doing fine
Steve shot someone, and he is doing time
He is up in Jersey somewhere
May sent you the enclosed card to tell you she
cares
I am doing great
I got a job in Philly decorating cakes

When we get married I can do our wedding cake
myself
The company I work for is going to send me to
school later to learn more stuff
It's good money, and it's something I love
And you won't have to do the drug-thang
Baby, things have changed
I got saved
I'm living for God now
When you get out we will get married
immediately, so we will not be doing wrong
I want us to really make it when you come home
We can have a good life doing right
It will take a minute, but we are strong
Baby, I will be waiting for you, and I am sincere
I 'm gonna do your time with you, and when you
get out I will still be here.

WHAT A BROKEN HEART CAN DO TO YOU

Love sounds so pretty
But when it fails it feels so gritty
There is nothing like having a broken heart
When you have a broken heart everything seems
broken
Love is gone, and you are alone with memories as
a token
It's funny how you can have twenty years of good
memories, and one bad memory can make you
forget them all
Especially, if it's the reason your love took a fall
A broken heart
Is truly nothing to play with or dispute about
A broken heart is something we all can do without
Your heart hurts
Your eyes are puffy from tears that trickled down
your face
No matter where you go, misery is present in your
space
You just don't want to do it again
"Let's just be friends"
That's your favorite line now
Because you have forgotten how
Love is
All you know about is a broken heart
Time hasn't come for you to let those memories
part
Trust me—you will remember what love feels like
And you will try again, giving it a better fight

I guess experiencing a broken heart is something
we all must go through
But we cannot give it the victory of making our
lives blue.

TREES

Passing through the trees
Never appreciating the true formation of their
leaves
Abuse them
Use them
Cut them down
When you know their goodness you will need
somehow
They give life to this world
Nourished from the soil
But they are taller than land
Complex so it takes wisdom and love to
understand
Their growth and why their roots are so strong
My conclusion, a tree is much like a woman
Never really appreciated and sometimes a victim of
wrong

WHAT THE WHITE MAN DON' DID NOW

My brotha you don't even know the struggle
You're only twenty-three
You're reaping the benefits of our ancestors of this
country
Now they went through hell
Stop complaining and get off your tail
I'm not saying that racism has ceased
But now you have a chance to accomplish your
dreams
Stand up and make a better way for someone else
Stop depriving yourself
Complaining about the white man isn't getting you
anywhere
Do something positive, and you wouldn't notice
the white man there
Because he can't hurt you
Not now
This time
This life
It's time to check yourself to make sure you are
doing right
Our ancestors died to make this happen
Education
Freedom of speech
Freedom to eat where we want to eat
We own houses
Big houses too
Businesses
Land
You don't have to fight now to prove that you are a
man
God made you that

You have no reason to be sitting home looking
dumb
MY BROTHA WE HAVE OVERCOME
So stop your negative thinking
Did you ever figure maybe you are the reason why
you keep sinking?

I AIN'T MISSING YOU AT ALL

I am the happiest I can be
Because I saved me
I love me
I am alone
No more troubles or evil spirits in my home
I ain't missing you at all Baby
If I were I would check myself into a hospital
because then I would know I am crazy
I ain't missing your everyday drinking
Or your jealous thinking
I ain't missing your fist up against my eye
Or your overbearing budget to get high
I ain't missing your disrespectful ways
And how you demand to stay out late
I ain't missing you at all
I ain't missing your sister when she calls our house
and tries not to speak
I ain't missing your mother who refuses to see you
are trifling
I ain't missing you at all
I can rest
It took me long enough to get this stress off my
chest
Baby, believe me when I say there are no tears
here
If you think I will be calling you
You are sadly mistaken
I have a new love in my life
And it's me!

LISA JANE HAS A BABY

Lisa Jane is having a baby, and it's sad
Because her uncle is the dad
She was only fifteen
Never had a chance to dream
Before he stole her virginity
The family covered up the dirty little secret when
it was revealed
But what it did to Lisa Jane took a long time to heal
They sent Lisa Jane away, but I don't know why
They should have put the uncle away or cast him
aside
Lisa Jane had her baby, and she never returned
home
She ran away from where they sent her and raised
her baby alone
She didn't contact her family until she was thirty-
two
She had raised her child and put herself through
school
Lisa Jane is a lawyer and doing her best
She overcame her circumstances and mastered her
tests
Lisa Jane having a baby at fifteen is true
But it never stopped her from doing what she had
to do
Lisa Jane proved she had grown to be a woman
hard as steel
Her strength and spirituality helped old wounds
heal.

THIS IS WHERE WE END

She hurt me
I thought she was my friend
But every time I turned around
She had a knife to my chin
I found out she tells everything I say
She envies my ways
And as a friend I loved her
Thought together we would grow old
It was a beautiful friendship to me, but to her it
was cold
Scheming and very vengeful she was
Full of venom inside—covered by a shallow shell
made of love
I had to let that friendship go
Ease away
I knew if I continued, she would cut me bad
someday
So long so-called friend
This is where we end
I watched closely and learned, yet I remained cool
I guess she thought I would keep on giving like I
was some fool.

...QUICKSAND

She's got her man
And she's happy
But she's happy with someone else's husband
He has no intentions of leaving his wife
And that's okay with her
As long as she has him in her life
But she doesn't know he and his wife are living
with HIV
She's manipulating and sneaky
She laughs at his wife and calls her a fool
But she will be the one who gets taken to school
She has been planted
So she thinks
But wait until she begins to sink
Time will go by fast
**As soon as she looks down and sees she's in
QUICKSAND**

He is the man
He copulates with all the girls
He's Captain Gigolo in his own world
Bony, Tinisha, and Felecia one night
Shonda, Tammy, and Kesha the next
But the disease called AIDS greeted him with one
of the ladies he met
He is planted
So he thinks
But wait until he begins to sink
Time will go by fast
**As soon as he looks down and sees he's in
QUICKSAND**

I'll take a little drink she said
While still in high school
Drinking a little liquor will kill her blues
Her mother does it from time to time
When her daddy's affairs are on her mother's
mind
But the girl began to drink more and more every
day
She is two steps from being an alcoholic and one
step from harm's way
She is planted
So she thinks
But wait until she begins to sink
Time will go by fast
**As soon as she looks down and sees she's in
QUICKSAND!**

DIFFERENCES

Don't hate who I am
Don't hate who I be
I thought you said you loved me
Well, this is me
You can't love half of me
You have to love all of me
And that includes things you can't and don't
understand
My idiosyncrasies
Baby, I am a man
A man who may not have grown up like you
I never lied to you
I always kept it real
I always told you the truth
You loved me then
Why don't you continue to love me now
You can't change me
I treat you good
I do everything under the sun and in the woods
For you
I can't impress your friends too
I speak; I am sociable
But I can't be what they want me to be
Can you be happy with me
You loved me before they said anything
Look, I know you were raised in the suburbs
Your friends have men with successful careers
And to you I cannot compete
Either you be happy with who I am

And who I be
Or set yourself free
You will never change me!

"You pray so hard for someone to love, and when you are
blessed with them you work so hard to change them. Did
you love the individual or all the changes you planned to
make?"

THE WORDS I LONG TO HEAR

Say that you love me
I need to hear those words
When I look into your eyes
I need to see your heart
I need to see your soul
Whenever I look at something I love
I think of you and the beautiful things you do
You brighten up my life
I have never felt this way before
You have truly opened a bolted door
My heart was closed to so many things
Then I met you
The healing you bring is so brand new
Say that you love me too
I need to hear those words
I long to hear those words
From you
And only you
If I don't hear them, I don't know what I would do
My world may become bolted again
Because I love you and you are the only one that
managed to get in
Say that you love me…
Please
You are what my world needs

...VAMPIRE

She sucks the life out of every man she meets
She's beautiful, and she appears to be so sweet
But she has no substance
None at all
She is looking for a money-clip or someone who is
ready to ball
You have to have a nice car to take her out
Money, money, money is what she is all about
She can't be a good friend
Because she is sneaky and heartless
She sinks her teeth into whomever she can
She will listen to the good things you say about
your man
And sneak in for the kill—soon as she gets her
chance
She will walk around you like she has done you no
wrong
When the man you had is now a part of her home
Her grip is worst than a pair of pliers
She moves like air in the night
Don't trust her—she's a vampire!

I AM RUNNING AWAY TO A BETTER PLACE

I don't feel in charge of me
I feel so alone
I can't think
Every room I run to there is someone there
Have you ever felt you were ugly?
Incomplete?
I don't know why I feel—I just feel certain ways
It doesn't matter what anyone else says
I feel so alone
I try so hard to blame it on my hormones
But I don't think it is
It is getting hard for me to live
I curl up in my bed in the middle of the day
Sometimes I lie on my back and stare at the ceiling
I don't know why
Don't ask me why
Don't make me feel crazy
I can see the look on your face
I knew you would never understand
That's why I am running away to a better place!

WHAT'S WRONG WITH ME

Why do I keep choosing the same kind of man?
What's wrong with me?
What's wrong with my pickin'?
They are never any good
At first they are
Then they change
Like milk curdles when it gets old
My good men soon turn to mold
Is it something wrong with me?
Is it my demeanor?
Why do I keep attracting the wrong man!
Why do they feel they have to lie to me?
I'm a magnet for the wrong men
God, this cycle must end!

SOBER

A clean house
The food that goes into my children's mouths
Sunshine
Clear skies
Rain
Broken chains
Hopes and dreams
Beautiful trees
Love
TV
The water in the deep blue sea
The boats that sail the ocean
The cars in motion
These are the things I now see that used to be a
blur
Everything is so clear, now that I live my life sober.

...THE LAW OF GRAVITY

I haven't looked into the mirror in a while
Today I took a long look
Noticed the lines in my smile
I am not as beautiful as I used to be
My skin sort of hangs on me
I look good for my age
But I am older I can tell
I never thought this day would come
Where my breast don't set up anymore
They are just here
And my legs are not as tight and firm as they used
to be
They have broken veins
I'm wearing the support hose I hated to see my
mother wear
Now I am happy to have a pair
My hands look dry all the time
I use so much lotion
With this arthritis, they hardly have any motion
And my eyes—I don't want to go there
It's an older more mature me
That has to embrace the law of gravity.

...HERE COMES THE RAIN

Sunny days are gone
And here comes the rain
I knew it would come, but I wasn't certain when
Did everything my way
Therefore, I can't complain
It's time for me to grow
I will take care of mine
I put up for the rainy days
I knew my skies would not always possess
sunshine
I have a real love in my life
He is here for me
And if I need to cry
I know where he will be
He'll insure me things are going to be okay
The rain will not wash my joy away
Here comes the rain
But the sun will come again

"Everyone has had drama in his or her life, but only few can put it into words."

Chapter Three

DRAMA SECTION

Everyone has a testimony before he or she becomes whoever God created him or her to be. A testimony is drama turned into God's masterpiece.

"Masterpieces belong to their Master."

SHE SLITHERS

She smiles, but her eyes are dark
Not to me
No, they are not the darkness a child your age can
see
Although she has legs, she doesn't walk
She slithers to me
I don't understand Big Sister
No, you don't
I see things others won't
In his ear her tongue moves slowly and speaks
crazy words
Things that you have never heard
She speaks English doesn't she, Big Sister
Yes, but she's not right
She tries to confuse us
You're sure Big Sister?
Yes, she does
She's got daddy fooled
Especially when she wiggles her hips
I hate to see her turn to him and lick her lips
She's trying to take mother's place
I see how when mother is not around she gets up
in daddy's face
What must we do Big Sister?
I don't know
I will think of something because mother's cousin
is stooping so low
She will not tear our family apart
Go to sleep Little Sister

| While your big sister stays on guard |

DENIAL

I have to hide every now and then, but it's okay
He doesn't hit me in my face
I mean—he is a man
Sometimes a man gets angry and hits his wife
Right?
He's not killing me
I mean, he pays all the bills
We have some good moments
All of our moments aren't bad
Trust me
Don't look at me like that—I am telling the truth
Okay, okay, he broke my leg once
But see, I misplaced his lunch
Look, I can't do any better
My kids are fed, and I don't want for a thing
He is a preacher
A man of God for heaven sake
God will soon tell him to stop hitting me
What else could I ask for?
You know that I don't have a high school
education
I was really blessed to get him
I'm really okay
What is a woman to do?
I would be nothing without him
Don't look at my hands shaking; I have had this
nervous condition for years
My husband loves me
Honest he does!

...BABY, DON'T CRY

SCENE: The lady's mother is sitting in a rocking chair. She is kneeled down by her mother's side crying.

Daughter:
She's very upset, and tears trickle from her eyes as she speaks.

Mama! Why you never told me about this pain he would cause me
You told me that there might be tears
You told me that he might do things I didn't quite agree with
But Mama you forgot to tell me this
Mama, you told me that there might be another woman someday
And sometimes it's better to forgive and just pray
But Mama what do I do about this
My husband was with his best friend, and his best friend is a man
Mama, can you relate because I can't understand
Was it something I did wrong
To make my man leave his home
For another hard muscular man
I don't know what to do
All I know is that I need you
Because Mama this is pain like no pain
This is pain that if I endure it alone, I know it will drive me insane
I have this image of my husband and his best friend in my head
My husband had his best friend in my bed

The lady dropped her head into her mother's lap as she cried aloud. Her mother said nothing as she stroked her daughter's head.

Shay Seven

I LAUGHED

Oh no! Please don't! I screamed!
But I could hear my flesh tear
He pushed and he pushed
No one else was there
Nooo! I screamed
But he never stopped
He just kept pushing and pushing
Until my bones popped
My ears hurt from my own screams
I think I became disoriented at some point to take
my mind away
When it tried to come back
I counted the squares on the ceiling and the cracks
that made the squares look like hats
I guess it lasted for about 10 minutes
I could feel my legs again once it was over
It was hard for me to lift my head since he pressed
his elbow in my throat to keep me still
Somehow I got up once he let me go
My entire body felt so'
I limped to my mother's room to this old dresser
she had
I walked back into the room where he claimed his
space in front of the TV
I thought it would be hard for me
But you know it wasn't hard at all
My finger felt so comfortable in such a little hole,
and I squeezed
I didn't even close my eyes

He would never hurt me anymore
Not unless he came in my dreams
I killed my stepfather at the age of fifteen
Pray for me!

MAMA, WHY DO YOU CRY?

Mama, why do you cry?
You put him out when he was barely a man
Told him you didn't want to see him anymore
All because of that red dress of yours he hung
behind his door
Mama, why do you cry?
I don't understand your tears
You told him last week when he tried to come to
visit you, to get the hell away from here
All because of his friend he rode with
Mama, I still don't know why you cry!
When so many times you closed your door
You told him he wasn't your son anymore
Now you cry because he is dead
When you went so far to be nasty because of the
life he led
I know why I cry
I cry because he was my brother
I loved him; I wasn't ashamed of him having a
man as his lover
Your tears I don't understand
You hated my brother all because he was a gay
man
No disrespect Mama, but I don't want to see your
tears
You should have loved my brother while he was
here
Mama, I want to comfort you because I know you
still must hurt—he was your child
But you were so hard on him when he tried so
desperately to make you smile
Mama, why do you cry?

Mother's response:

I cry because he was my son
I carried him for nine months
How dare you question me
I was a loving mother to both of you
But I am a Christian woman who couldn't
compromise
Do you know how many nights I cried
Do you know how many nights I prayed
That he would get his life right and turn from his
sinful ways
I cry because my blood flowed through his veins
And seeing him turn away from Christ caused me
much pain
I never hated him, but I didn't know how to love
him anymore
With him gallivanting with his lover all around
town
Hurting God's heart and bringing God's Kingdom
down
That is why I cry
I cry because I couldn't help my child
No matter what I did—no matter how hard I tried
That is why I cry!

A MAN

He said he is a man because he was a sperm donor
of three kids
He said he is a man because of all the gangbanging
he did
He is straight thugged-out he said
I guess that is supposed to sound good to you and I
But when I hear it—it makes me want to cry
Because to me what he is saying is that he will
never change
Things in his life will remain the same
He will never work an honest job
Because to him working an honest job makes his
life too hard
He will die with his tattoos on his chest
With dope in his pockets and leaving his
"baby's mama" stressed
He said he is a man
However, he doesn't know that being a man is
more than making kids he doesn't take care of
Being a man is more than showing his gang
members love
Being a man is saying I was once thugged-out
But now that life for me is over because I know
what living is all about
THAT'S A MAN
And I wish more males would understand!

MESSY SITUATION

I never meant for things to be this way
I really didn't
She has hair so soft
Soft as velvet I tell you
I will not even mention the smell
Her body isn't perfect at all
But it was her essence
When she moved she shined
When she sat down and crossed her legs, chills
took over my spine
I told her I wasn't married before I knew it
God, now I am in deep
I love my wife, but for this lady I am so weak
I don't know how to get out of this thing I have
created
My mistress—though she doesn't know she is—
wants to marry me
How can I tell her that I just—
I mean how
I don't know
I don't want to break her heart
And honestly I love her so
But I am already taken

Shay Seven

TEN YEARS

He hears the sound of someone struggling to break
free
The sounds of his friend's flesh breaking and the
clattering of his teeth
He uses a pillow to cover his ears to stop the
sounds that are so near
He is tired of this place
He feels trapped in such a small space
Family he doesn't hear from much
They are too busy, so they don't keep in touch
He cries sometimes when the lights go off
He wishes he was an angel, so he could break free
Maybe a butterfly so during recreational time he
could fly in a tree
Veracity is, seems like he will spend forever behind
the bars of this place
Eating tasteless food which leaves a frown on his
face
The bars make him feel alone
He wishes he could take back his crime and go
home
He is young and lost, and sometimes he wishes he
would die
He lost his freedom trying to take someone else's
piece of the pie.

SHE'S LIVING THE GOOD LIFE

First woman:

She has jewels on her wrist worth more than my
house
She stays sharp as can be
Did you see her car, honey
That girl got some money
She is living the good life
Girl, she got her stuff together tight
I heard her house is worth more than 400,000
dollars
She dates men no lower than white collar

Second woman:

Yeah, but I heard she stays on her knees
With her mouth she does unspeakable things
Men go in and out of the big house she has
She pays a terrible price with her body for that Jag
I don't envy her at all
Because ol' girl stays on call
She holds her head up in the day
But at night I bet she cries for a better way

Pray for her

HYPOCRITE

Stop pointing your finger judging everyone else
You know you are not all that you claim to be
Smiling in church and running around kissing the
pastor's feet
You and your husband look really happy, but you
don't crave his touch
You use every curse word when you express how
you hate his guts
At church you're Sister So and So
At the hotel with your boyfriend, you're a sister
who won't say no
Your husband doesn't know about your boyfriend
And how you and he do it again and again
How is it so easy for you to point your finger
When you are intimate with a man who isn't your
husband
See, you walk around town shaking your head at
other people
When you know your sins are greater or just as
equal
So don't come my way trying to judge me
Because I will beat you up with words
Demolish you with things you've never heard
You're not worth one red cent
And your life is a bottomless pit
You're nothing but a no-good hypocrite!

DAMNATION
{Short screenplay}

FADE IN
EXT. THE PARK-EVENING
It is a beautiful summer day in Atlanta. Fallon is sitting in the parking staring out at the trees as she often does when she likes to relax. Terry walks down to her.

> TERRY
> (He walks down and sits next to Fallon)
> Hey.

> FALLON
> (She turns to him and smiles)
> What's up? How did you
> know where I was?

> TERRY
> I know where you come when
> you want peace.

> FALLON
> (She giggles)
> You think you know me so
> well. You look nice. Where
> are you coming from?

> TERRY
> I got the job at the church.

> FALLON
> (Excited)
> What! Man, I am so proud of
> you! You are just doing it!
> You will have your MDIV
> soon, and you got the job as

FALLON (Continued)
>the church pastor. I am so
>proud of you!

TERRY
>I know you are. I am really
>happy right now. It is a small
>church, and there are not
>many people in the
>congregation. I know I can
>grow it. Although it is small,
>they are still going to start me
>off with sixty grand a year.

FALLON
>What! You are just doing it!
>I always knew you were
>going to be a success. (She
>turns away and looks out at
>the trees).

TERRY
(Pulling a ring out)
>What good is success if you
>cannot share it with your best
>friend? (He turns to her and
>gets on one knee with a ring.)
>Fallon, will you share my life
>with me? I need you by my
>side.

FALLON
(Looking down at him)
>Terry, I am happy for you.
>But we went over this before.
>You said it yourself; I am your
>best friend.

TERRY
People marry their best
friends most of the time.
Those make the best
marriages. Everything is good
for me, and I need us to be
good.

FALLON
Do you even love me Terry
like I love you?

TERRY
(He drops his head and lifts it back up.)
How could you ask me
something like that? I love
you Fallon. I have not been a
perfect man. But I knew
whenever I decided to get
married you would be the
woman. (Pause) Come on
Fallon, say yes. You know we
are good together. There will
be nothing that we will not
accomplish. You always have
my back.

FALLON
Will I be the only one?

TERRY
Come on now, I am a man of
God.

FALLON
You were a man of God two
years ago. Have you given up
all your old ways Terry?

TERRY

Fallon, would I be asking you to marry me right now? Why do you act like you don't love me?

FALLON

I love you. I have always loved you, even when you decided to love me late. I don't want to be hurt because you think you have to have a wife by your side to preach to these people or to make your picture complete. I want you to love me. Really love me Terry!

TERRY

What is wrong with you! I just told you I love you. (Calming down) Baby I know I have hurt you, but this time is the right time. I am for real. Don't leave me hanging. I would be lost without you. You didn't go to college, but you encouraged me to go to college. I am in a Master's program because you knew I could do it. Now baby I want to help you with some of your dreams. You have had a hard life. Let me make it easier. (He kisses her lips.) What do you say?

FALLON

Yes, yes! I love you Terry.

> TERRY
> That's my girl. (He puts the
> ring on her finger and hugs
> her).

CUT TO
EXT. OUTSIDE-IN THE PARK- AFTERNOON
Lauren and Fallon are exercising. They are doing crunches
and Fallon starts talking.

> FALLON
> Something happened to me
> yesterday.

> LAUREN
> What? You met a man?

> FALLON
> Well something like that,
> Terry asked me to marry him.

> LAUREN
> (She jumps up)
> What! Are you serious?

> FALLON
> (Still doing her crunches)
> Yes! I couldn't believe it
> myself.

> LAUREN
> Let me see the ring! I know
> you said yes. You love him so
> much.

> FALLON
> (Shows her the ring)
> I do. He said that he really
> loves me too.

LAUREN
Girl, I am so happy for you.
You should be more excited.

FALLON
I am excited. It's just that
Terry has a past, and I just
want to make sure that it is all
over.

LAUREN
All men have a past Fallon.
Come on now. He did not
meet you coming out of the
womb. Terry is a preacher!
Graduated from one of the
best colleges and he is now
working on his Masters. Girl,
you would have to be a fool to
pass him up! Our mother did
not raise any fools. He is
doing something with his life.
You have been there for this
man. Do not let some other
woman profit off your hard
work. You encouraged him
in the middle of the night.
You took him lunch and
helped him with his laundry
while he was in college. I
thought you were crazy, but
it paid off for you. I am
happy for my sister.

FALLON
Thank you. I am happy. I
just want to make sure I am
doing the right thing.

> LAUREN
> You are. Mama had a hard time raising us. You have a man that is going to make sure you never have to go through what Mama went through. We should be celebrating. I am going to give you a little party. It will be fun.

> FALLON
> No, no don't make a big fuss over me getting married.

> LAUREN
> I am not, but we need to have a party. My sister is getting married!

CUT TO
EXT. BASKETBALL COURT-EVENING
Terry and a group of guys are playing basketball. Fallon walks up to Terry and brings him a clean shirt. She gets stunned when she sees Terry's ex-lover on the court.

> TERRY
> (Stops playing ball and runs up to Fallon)
> What are you doing here baby?

> FALLON
> I know you said you were playing ball today, so I thought I would bring you something to drink and an extra shirt. I wasn't doing anything. Maybe you and I can get a bite to eat.

Lonnie stares at Fallon and Terry causing Fallon to notice him.

> TERRY
> Thank you baby, but it's just a quick game. The fellows and I were going to go out to eat.

> FALLON
> (Upset and shocked)
> What is he doing here?

> TERRY
> (Acting oblivious)
> Who?

> FALLON
> Him! You know who I am talking about!

> TERRY
> (Taking Fallon over to the side so no one will hear her)
> Baby, calm down. He is one of the fellows.

> FALLON
> Are you still seeing him? Terry, you will not do this to me!

> TERRY
> Baby, will you calm down. The other guys do not know about what happened between

TERRY (Continued)
Lonnie and me. And I do not
want them to know. So lower
your voice.

FALLON
I don't want him in my life
Terry. If you are going to
have him in our lives I will
not marry you! You said you
changed.

TERRY
I have changed! Those days
are gone baby. I am all yours.
I promise. (He grabs her chin
and looks into her eyes.)
Don't act like this. I am
marrying you. (Pause) You
got me. (He kisses her lips).

CUT TO
INT. SHELIA'S PLACE-EVENING
Fallon is talking to her friends as they drink champagne.

SHELIA
What's up with you? I feel
that your heart is heavy.

FALLON
I am okay. I was just
thinking.

SHELIA
'Bout what? You know how
we do—spill it.

FALLON
> Terry asked me to marry him,
> and I said yes.

DARLECIA
> That's great!

SHELIA
(Nonchalant)
> He must have got that job. So
> what does this mean, Fallon?

DARLECIA
> It means she is getting
> married. That is what it
> means!

SHELIA
> Baby shut up, she knows what
> I am talking about. That dude
> aint straight! He will never
> be straight! You guys making
> some sort of deal or somthin'?

FALLON
> No. You know I would never
> marry for the wrong reasons.
> I love Terry. He is the first
> person I would want to spend
> the rest of my life with.

SHELIA
> So what is he going to do with
> his man? I went to college
> with the brotha. He was my
> friend before you were my
> friend. I know him. He
> doesn't deserve you.

DARLECIA
You are disrespecting God,
Shee.

SHELIA
(Tipsy)
I aint disrespecting God. He
disrespecting God! His gay
ass. (Looking up in the sky)
Not you God, but Terry is the
gay ass. (Looking down at
Darlecia) Yeah, I said it.

DARLECIA
You and I are gay Shee. Gay
people shouldn't pastor
churches?

SHELIA
I don't know about all that,
but if you are going to be gay,
be gay! Don't try to cover it
up with a wife. Fallon knows
I am telling the truth. Terry is
my dude, but I do not like
what he is doing. I know he
hasn't changed. He is playing
with God. There are some
churches out here that allow
you to be gay and pastor—
hell go join them.

FALLON
How do you figure he is
playing with God? He has
changed in a lot of ways.

SHELIA
He will have his Masters, and
he has a church now. Oh
and he is getting ready to
have a wife. I mean don't get
me wrong the brotha loves
God. He prayed for lots of
people in college and even
today. Fallon, you were
always a good girl at his beck
and call. You deserve
something real. Terry cannot
give you that.

FALLON
What we have is real.

SHELIA
More on your part than on
his part. You don't have to
listen to me. I am just saying,
how can you grow in a
church when your pastor has
a wife and a boyfriend? God
knows the truth, and the truth
is Terry is still sleeping with
men while he uses you as a
facade. Hey, I am down for
whatever. Let's toast to the
preacher's wife. (She lifts her
glass in the air).

DARLECIA
Don't be sarcastic Shelia; this
is serious. She has had too
much wine Fallon.

SHELIA
> Don't blame it on the wine! I
> say what I want to say with or
> without the wine! Who the
> hell you think I am! I'm
> Shelia! She knows I am
> serious. I don't know if what
> we are doing is right, but I
> damn sho' know what they
> are about to do is wrong. I
> was the one who told her
> about Lonnie when Terry and
> I were in undergrad. I aint
> coming to his damn church.
> I don't want to be standing
> by his ass when lightning
> strikes.

FALLON
> I better go.

SHELIA
> You don't have to go because
> of me. I mean I am just real
> mixed with a little wine. I
> have found the two don't mix.
> I keep losing friends when the
> wine comes out.

DARLECIA
> Fallon, if you love him and
> you believe him, marry him.
> You know Shee; she talks too
> much. What if I would have
> listened to the people who
> told me not to be with her? I
> wouldn't be happy today.

FALLON
Thank you Darlecia.

SHELIA
Sure thank Darlecia because
she said what you want to
hear. Make me the enemy.

DARLECIA
Fallon, if you love him let him
love you.

CUT TO
EXT. OUTSIDE IN THE PARK-EVENING
Fallon is sitting down looking up as she talks aloud to God.

FALLON
(Soliloquy)
God, I know you are out
there. I just don't know what
to do. I love this man. He is a
Godly man like I prayed for,
but I don't know if he has
really changed his
homosexual behavior. He is
anointed. I mean the man
can preach demons out of
people—the boy can preach.
People really believe in him. I
will be proud to be his wife,
First Lady Thomas. It sounds
good to me. He has to lose
Lonnie. I know I am not
marrying him if he does not
lose Lonnie. He says he loves
me God, and he wants to give
me a chance to live my
dreams. I am just so
confused. I don't know

FALLON (Continued)
>
> whether I should love him
> and believe him or love him
> and leave him. God if he is
> the man for me please give
> me some kind of sign.
> Anything God! I want
> something that is real.

CUT TO
INT. CHURCH~SANCTUARY~AFTERNOON
Terry and Fallon are standing in front of the pastor getting
married. The camera shows Fallon's maid of honor and
moves slowly to Fallon and Terry. Finally the camera
shows Terry's best man, **Lonnie**. In the background you
hear the wedding music. The camera gets a full view of the
wedding party then it **BLACKS OUT!**

The End

"Unconditional love is the manifestation of God. Therefore, when you walk in unconditional love God is with you."

Chapter Four

ROMANCE SECTION

Romance is special when it is expressed beautifully. We were created to love, and anything else is unnatural. You may refer to the "Song of Solomon" in the Bible.

"When God created a woman for a man, he actually gave the man a taste of heaven on earth."

HEAVEN HAS A GHETTO

Brotha, you asked the question
Does heaven have a ghetto
Quite frankly, I think the answer to your question
is yes
But maybe it should be the other way around
Does the ghetto have a heaven?
Why yes it does
Sweet brown, brown, and strong
Welcoming the ghetto king to sit proudly on her
throne
All guns down please
Leave all drugs alone
HEAVEN has a motion as smooth as the waves in
the ocean
A heart as big as the sea
Skin so silky smooth on her body
Yes, **HEAVEN** is made of flesh
Heaven will be there through thick and thin
Loving you when you're not at your best
HEAVEN
Can you get in?
All you have to do is treat her right
Respect the territory
Listen to and understand her plight
Don't neglect her struggle or leave her beautiful
garden when you feel it's too hard to be good
Instead, embrace **"HEAVEN"** and for her do all you
could

Yes my brotha, the ghetto does have a heaven right
here on earth
You don't have to die to have her or experience a
rebirth
Just embrace her without pollution
Don't bring her down to destitution
Heaven is truly **HEAVEN**
Have you properly addressed her yet?
She was made for you to enjoy and love
HEAVEN was sent to you from God up above!

...MY HUSBAND

I don't have to tell him what to do
He knows
If I am too tired and the house needs cleaning
He does it
He surprises me with gifts frequently
And he doesn't hesitate to tell me that he loves me
He works, and we put our money together
We share our goals and dreams with each other
He helps me, and I help him
He knows the right things to say when my light
appears dim
Doesn't get his kicks out of seeing me hurt
He believes in God and doesn't mind going to
church
He is not very religious but neither am I
As long as he believes in God and applies God's
word to his life, that's fine
Treasures his marriage and believes in fidelity
until his death
He doesn't have to say it—you can tell it by how he
carries himself
He doesn't lie to me even if he feels the truth may
hurt my heart
He gives it to me straight; I don't have to spend an
hour picking him apart
When we are mad with each other we make up
with no problem
We don't hold grudges; we communicate
Communication helps us make fewer mistakes
He doesn't eyeball other women in my view
He respects me constantly without me telling him
what to do

Treats me like the Queen I am
And I treat my baby like a King
He is my soul mate and my everything!

…HERE COMES THIS LOVE THANG

I don't feel like being in love anymore
I just don't!
Sometimes love plays games
Get you all riled up when it turns out not to be
worth a "thang"
Makes you smile and feel so free
And breaks your heart as soon as it flees
LOVE, LOVE, LOVE
That mess is for the birds
So I used to say
I have been by myself
And being alone to me is somewhat like death
I like the long walks in the park as we hold hands
I enjoy us walking on the beach—barefoot in the
sand
My lips upheave automatically for your kiss
When you are away it's something my lips miss
Baby, I love you, and I am not ashamed
When I saw you walking I said to myself, "Mm,
here comes this love thang."

HOW DO YOU FEEL

You are consuming me, and it's funny because we
don't spend a lot of time together
However, I find myself fantasizing about being
with you forever
Your personality is intriguing to me
It's your soft touch that makes me want you so
much
You make me glow inside-out
The way you make me feel is what living is all
about
See, you affect me positively and make me act a
certain way
And I love the way you make me act and how my
feelings for you give me so much to say
You give me grace
You leave a massive smile on my face
You put a tingle in my toes
Make hair stand up wherever it grows
Is this just that new feeling I ask myself
Or will it stay
I'm so scared to even try again
I'm running although I want to let you in
Will you appreciate me for who I am
Love me when no one else cares
Or will you crumble my heart very slow
Laugh with your friends about how I love you so
Will you be true and see my soul when you look
into my eyes
Will you be faithful and tell me no lies

These are just the things I feel inside
How do you feel; I need to know
I'm holding on, and I don't want to let go.

YOU'RE THE BEST THING THAT EVER HAPPENED TO ME

It's so hard to tell you how I feel
Let me start by telling you that my love for you is
real
Your love for me helps my heart beat, and our
longevity encourages me
The love I have for you no words or cards can
really express
You are the love of my life—my wife and my
mistress
You brighten up my pathway
You are the only woman that I will love and
cherish until my dying day

I'LL KNOW WHEN YOU LOVE ME

I will know when you love me
Although it will be nice to hear, you won't have to
say it
I will feel it in your spirit
The pupils of your eyes when I come around will
turn into my face
You will light up when I enter your space
Your soul will intertwine with mine
Your bottomless pit will be no more, and your
skies will possess sunshine
You will never want to see or bring a tear to my
eyes
Although you're not perfect, for me you will try
And I will love you for all your efforts and
dedication
Baby, I will know when you love me, and there
will be no mistaking.

A WONDERFUL FRIEND LIKE YOU

You have truly been there in my time of need
You really understand what friendship means
Never have you betrayed me when I needed you so
You make everything seem so much better when I
need you the most
There has never been a time I wouldn't do the
same for you
When you hold out your hand, I will pull you
through
That is why our friendship works so well
Loving each other unconditionally will make sure
our friendship will never fail

BABY LISTEN

I truly miss you
Your touch
I love you much
I think about how you made me feel
Would it hurt for you to know the deal?
Would it?
Could it?
You're supposed to be untouchable
Your heart
Your soul
I think you felt me reaching
You felt me
And you ran because you are a man—not ready
Ran to a place you thought you were safe
But you are safe with me
Loving you is easy
Said you don't need me
Maybe not
Not maybe
But ***I'M LOVE***
A breath of fresh air into your lungs
A solid beat added to your heart
I am life and that more abundantly
I bring my friends, **HAPPINESS AND PEACE**
We will put your soul at *EASE*
No more hiding
We found you!!
Now rest…
Rest and enjoy this thing called **LOVE**
Enjoy the **PEACE** and **HAPPINESS** it brings
For we were sent by a much *HIGHER BEING*

DELUSIONAL

I walked along the beach
Sand massaged my bare feet
Sky so blue and beautiful
Air so crisp
It clears my lungs
Soft gentle mist
Chill bumps running down my spine
From the coolness of the air
Sounds of birds here and there
My hair blows
Dreads shoulder length
Day so beautiful
Heaven sent
I looked ahead
Ten feet or more perhaps
And I saw this sculpture
Sculpture I couldn't have done better sculpting
myself
Hair short but velvety black
Two-piece hugging curves that…
Made me say MERCY
Beautiful reddish-brown skin tone I had never
seen before
An intoxicating swing in her motion
Similar to the smoothness of the waves in the
ocean
Her presence made my tongue automatically
moisten my lips
I looked down for a minute—didn't want to keep
staring at the swing in her hips

When we pass, I have to say something I thought
to myself
When I looked up again my perfection
disappeared
Where did she go?
I looked around
I saw her nowhere
Vanished into thin air
Did I see her
Or was she in my head
This is very unusual
I feel so **DELUSIONAL.**

...YOU ARE MY AND I AM YOUR DESTINY

I am in love with you
And for me that means forever and a day
I look forward to staying home cuddled up with
you late
I look forward to us just jumping in the car driving
without a clue
Holidays with your beautiful smile
Holding each other for long periods of time
Without saying a word
Spending money because we are making it
Fat bank account, withdrawing a million couldn't
break it
Even when times don't seem so bright
We get closer and have deeper communication
instead of fight
No one can say a word against my husband to me
And that's the way it supposed to be
Even if you are wrong
Still I have my baby's back
And trust me I won't let a soul forget that
It's me for you and you for me
We are soul mates; you are my destiny
The water in my sea
The sand on my beach
The blood flowing to my heart
No one or nothing will tear us apart
God said it's so
So it shall be
God is our "glue"

And I am yours and you are my destiny!

WORK OF ART

The moon shines down on my summer home
As the wind blows generously
I open the glass doors just a little
So that as I love your body you can feel the wind
blow across your back
A blanket accompanied by a bottle of champagne
chilled to perfection
We will toast to our union and take only a sip
After the sip, I will be tasting its sweetness from
your lips
Beautiful Mahogany you are
Your beautiful skin makes me in a hurry to
undress you
With every piece of garment I remove
I press my lips against you
Your body is a "work of art"
My museum is where I want it to be forever with
me
Imperfection or whatever it may be
I love you for you
You have been here throughout all
My crown that makes me king
My hope that makes me dream
When I look into your eyes
I feel good about my prize
I know I have done extremely well
So I pause
Nothing is wrong
I have to look at you intricately
Yes, I have done well

No, no let me stop
God has done well
You are a blessing from the sky that overlooks
where we lay
Can't take the glory—I must give it to the one and
only **DIVINE**
For blessing me with a wife so irresistibly
beautiful, sweet, and kind.

The End

"Life is too great to live like it is too short."

TITLES COMING SOON BY SHAY 7

Everyone Has a Testimony Vol. 1 (Novel)
"Why You Make My Brown Eyes Blue"
April 2012
$16.95

A Diversified Black Woman Vol. 2
"I was…I am the Face of…"
August 2012
$23.00

Everyone Has a Testimony Vol. 2 (Novel)
"Lemonade"
December 2012
$16.95

Children's Collection
Junebug and Jay
February 2013

Shaytales
P.O. Box 115448
Atlanta, Georgia 30310
www.shaytales.com